The ghostwriter

A Novella

KAIRA LOCKWOOD

Editing by Kimberly Huther of Wordsmith Editing
Website: wordsmith-editing.com

Formatting by Kaira Lockwood
Cover Photo by Kaira Lockwood
Cover Design by Kaira Lockwood
Copyright © 2024 by Kaira Lockwood.
All rights reserved.

First Print and Electronic Edition: 2024

Embrace life without any regrets. Learn from life's lessons and cherish its blessings.

Chapter 1

Isabel

I ran my fingers along the rustic dining table and admired the décor of Zetta Castellan. Her mix of portraits, dried flowers, candles, books, and trinkets felt like a veil of romantic nostalgia. The smelled of a mixture of dark, buttery rum cider and fresh cloves with a hint of apple cinnamon; a very luxurious, passionate, and heartwarming fragrance. Even though I didn't know her, I felt an immediate connection. It's no wonder her words alone gripped and entranced the hearts and souls of readers around the world.

"Do you have any questions, Ms. Isabel?"

I turned to smile at the lady who had given me a tour of the tiny one-bedroom cabin and shared some of what she knew about Zetta, the late prolific and prestigious writer.

Iris Doherbleek was a thin, older woman who stood about five-feet-two-inches. I guess this height, because I only stand five-feet-four-inches. Her silver hair was perfected in a tight bun that predominately displayed her dark ends and tinsel-gray roots, which appeared to sparkle when she turned her head towards the light. Aside from her captivating hair color, her makeup was flawlessly modest and elegant, with a noble contrast of red lipstick. Dressed in business attire, she held tight to her chest a worn, leather-cased journal filled with Zetta's end-of-life notes, some of which she was instructed to share with me.

"No, Iris, I think you've explained everything." I smiled at her. "It's a lot. I have to admit that. A little overwhelming, but I'll be fine. I'm sure after a few days of staying here, I'll be feeling right at home."

"Well, that's exactly what Zetta would want—for you to feel at home."

She smiled, and stared at me as if waiting for a response. After a long awkward silence, I inhaled the luxuriant aroma and glanced around the cabin. It felt like I'd walked into a time capsule. Shadow boxes of best-selling books, quotes, awards, photos, and canvas prints lined the walls. In the main living area adjacent to the fireplace, a floor-to-ceiling bookshelf lined the entire wall. Hardcovers, paperbacks, and journals dressed these shelves. According to Iris, this bookshelf was exclusively the work of Zetta. It was her clandestine collection of words. Every book she had crafted pridefully aligned the shelves, alongside awards. In place of bookends, stacks of her handwritten, intimate journals veined the shelves. Each stack was topped with a devil's ivy plant with leaves that trailed down the shelf edges. Iris noted it was one of Zetta's favorite plants, as it not only symbolized wealth, good fortune, perseverance and eternity, but remained green forever, even when kept in the dark, and was impossible to kill.

In the four-season porch, bookshelves lined the bottom half walls, while sheer white curtains enhanced the towered windows—giving an open, airy, and elegant feeling. On top of the bookshelves sprawled framed portraits, block quotes, candles, trinkets, and more devil's ivy plants.

Zetta was adamant about getting only signed editions by authors she loved and adored. Well-known for traveling to other authors' book signings, she wasn't timorous with her love for indie authors. She expressed significant views on how many of their stories should have been on the big screen and, at minimal, scaling the best-seller lists.

I glanced at the stack of paperbacks displayed on the nearby glass coffee table. *Our Daily Moments* by Nancy Kuykendall was the top paperback. After a brief second glance at the other paperbacks, I noticed they were all written by that same author. How cool to have an entire table dedicated to you in another author's home! I would have plenty of time to peek further into this stack of coffee table books. And maybe it would give me more insight into who Zetta was, and not just through online interviews, vlogs, blogs, and film reels.

"You know, I do have one question." I repositioned the strap on my shoulder and gazed at Iris. "I guess I'm still wondering why she chose me to write her biography or memoir. I'm a little confused about that one."

Iris smiled and shrugged her shoulders. She took a breath, and I thought she was going to speak but she hesitated. Her smile faded as she glanced around the room then back to me.

"There are some questions we don't have answers to, and that would be one of them. I know a lot about her, but there's also a lot I don't know. She was a very private person. Especially later in life. So, unfortunately, I don't have that answer. I was just designated to contact you and give you her instructions upon her death. But maybe you'll find your answer to that question in some of her journals." She forced a short smile and glanced over at Zetta's personal bookshelf.

I nodded at her response, wondering what part of my question seemed to bother her.

"Yeah. Aside from myself, I've never known anyone who was a daily journal writer. And based on her bookshelves filled with them, I can only assume she never missed a day. I hope one day my journals will look as nice as hers on my shelves."

"Any other questions, Ms. Isabel?"

"No. I think I'll get myself acquainted here. I just hope I make her proud. Writing a memoir is a huge project to undertake, especially when you don't know the person you're writing about."

"Like I said earlier, Ms. Isabel, this cabin is just as she left it. All her belongings and writings are here. The binder she left for you should help you ease into the role she wanted you to fill. Regardless, I know she'll be proud of your work." She winked. "From talking with you, you and Zetta would've gotten along very well. She chose the right person."

I waved to Iris as she drove down the driveway. The click of the gate closing sent a mini jolt of panic through my body. I was alone in a cabin in the middle of the Northwoods. Although an iron fence and security cameras surrounded the property, being in the home of a woman who had passed less than two months earlier made me a little uncomfortable.

There was a house on the other side of the fence. According to Iris the owners rarely visited the house, as they used it as a vacation home. There wasn't much mentioned in Zetta's final notes about the neighbors, so Iris assumed they also kept to themselves.

Zetta was a homebody. Iris had said. She never liked to leave her house. Some people's happy places are their gardens, or places to drive to for solitude. Not Zetta. Her happy place was her cabin and keeping to herself. I doubt she ever met the neighbors.

I walked back onto the porch and admired her choice of white wicker furniture, all dressed in cushions and matching throw blankets. The wicker end tables and matching coffee table each had a glass top with themed centerpieces and stacks of curated books. It felt like I was standing in a home and garden magazine shoot. In the air was a nostalgic, warm feeling of love and romance in abundance. I doubt one could stand here and not sense that welcoming feeling. But there was also a mysterious and intriguing aura surrounding the place. And I couldn't wait to learn more about the woman who had graced these rooms just a few short weeks ago.

In lieu of pinching myself to make sure I wasn't dreaming of standing in the home of Zetta Castellan, I laughed, shook my head, and thanked her out loud for choosing me to write her story. People are closer to you in death than in real life, so I knew she could hear me. There was also a good chance she was standing here with me in this very room.

A shiver ran up my spine at the thought of that, and I had to bring myself back to positive and uplifting thoughts. Alone in a new place, in the middle of nowhere, being scared out of my mind wasn't how I wanted to spend my first night. It was also not the impression I wanted Zetta to have of me. I would be the perfect houseguest, put myself into the life she once lived, and make her proud of her decision to choose me for this project.

I brought my suitcases and bags in from the car, took a nice shower, had some dinner, then stood before Zetta's bookcase. There were so many journals, it was hard to know where to start. Then I remembered the partial manuscript in the back of the binder that Iris had directed my attention to earlier. Per Zetta's instructions in the leather binder that Iris read from, I was to start with the manuscript in the back of the binder.

I made myself some hot chai, grabbed the binder, and got comfortable on the loveseat in the living room in front of the fireplace. I opened the binder and flipped to the back section. After I read the first page of the manuscript, I grabbed a throw blanket and set my drink on the coffee table. One page and I was already fused to the words of Zetta Castellan.

Chapter 2

Zetta

I glanced up at the woman smiling before me, opened the cover of the book, and grabbed my marker.

"I just love your books, Mrs. Castellan," she blurted, a big grin on her face. "I binge-read every book of yours. And now I have a bookcase for your books only, in my dining room. I have every paperback and hardcover book. Even the international covers." She beamed as she spoke.

"Well, I sure love to hear you're enjoying my stories. And thank you for the support and for granting me an entire bookcase. That's so sweet. I appreciate that, Rebecca," I replied as I read her name on the sticky note.

When she saw the signed book, her eyes lit up with joy.

"Thank you so much for coming tonight. I hope to see you again."

"Oh, yes!" she exclaimed as she carefully placed the signed copy in her canvas bag. "I'll be at your next New York signing. Well, I'll be at all of them.

Thank you again, Mrs. Castellan. I'm so glad I got to meet you. You're an incredible person, and truly made my night."

Reaching for the next person's book my smile faded, and I was taken aback. My heart momentarily stopped, and I had to remind myself to breathe. As I looked into his eyes, maroon flushed my face.

"Zetta."

Like a wave of emotions, his comforting voice immersed me in memories of tailgate nights, falling stars, and silk sheets. Even though I'd written hundreds of books, his presence left me speechless. I stared at him with a yearning, throbbing desire to race around the table and into his arms. I couldn't shake the memories of him hoisting me up and spinning us around, my laughter filling the air as I held on to his neck.

"Out of all your books, this is definitely one of my favorites," he said, winking and gesturing towards it, his eyes fixed on mine.

"Right. Um... Hi."

His kiss. His touch. His arms wrapped around me as he told me everything was going to be okay. His words—

"I apologize if I'm making you feel uncomfortable," he whispered, glancing at a few individuals nearby, then back to me.

"You aren't." I hesitated. "Okay. Maybe a little. But in a good way." I nodded and fumbled with the marker in my hand before shaking my head. "You just caught me off guard."

I stared at the post-it with his name on it and glanced back up at him.

"Um..."

"Jed. I still go by Jed Conley."

I grinned, let out a small laugh, shook my head, and signed his book.

I cleared my throat and shifted my attention back to him. "Well, Mr. Conley, it is very nice to see you. A lovely surprise." I took another deep breath as he held his hand over mine for a few seconds before taking his book.

"You as well. Take care, Zetta." He winked as he walked away, not looking back. I kept my gaze fixed on him until the door of the bookstore closed.

The fact that there weren't many people in line behind Jed Conley was a good thing, considering the rest of the signing was a blur. All I could think about was him. It took everything in me to not race out of the store after him. The sound of my name on his lips awakened buried memories and emotions. He had a way of captivating me, and he knew it.

What was he doing here? This signing was in New York—quite a drive from Wisconsin, where I had last known him to live. It had been years since I last saw him. Decades, to be honest. He crossed my mind daily, but him showing up at one of my book signings all these years later was an unexpected and pleasant surprise.

For years, I had to conceal all the feelings of us within me. Only my books provided an outlet for their release. I wondered if he read my books and, if he did, how thoroughly. Did he grasp the implied message in my words? He left me with an over-whelming need to let my emotions out, and writing provided the safest release.

"I can finish up here if you want to get back home for an early night. It's been a long day," Catherine, my assistant, said as she boxed up the few remaining hardcover books.

"Are you sure? I can stay and help. You've been working all day, too, and shouldn't have to do all this by yourself."

"I'm not by myself, remember?" She giggled as she nudged my arm.

"Oh!" I laughed. "I'm so sorry. I forgot you brought your fiancé on this trip with us. Well, I didn't actually forget. I knew he was here all weekend. It was just a moment of brain fog."

"We'll get things packed up. You head home. Get some rest and we'll see you back in Wisconsin at some point."

"Okay. Thank you so much, Catherine. You've been a lifesaver. And I couldn't have pulled any of this off without you. The back room is still open for anything extra to go, and I'll stop back this week to—"

"Goodnight, Zetta!" She laughed.

After grabbing my bag, I thanked her again and left the store.

The night was warm, almost on the edge of muggy, but the breeze made it the perfect evening for a walk. I was glad my condo wasn't too far from this bookstore. Although a walk seemed pleasant I was exhausted from the busy weekend, and the idea of going to bed early sounded heavenly.

"Can I walk you to wherever you're staying?"

I turned around quickly.

"Jed!" I smiled as he embraced me in one of his

hugs. "I didn't know if I would see you again."

"Don't think for one second I flew to New York just to have you sign a book and then disappear without a proper goodbye."

"What are you doing all the way over here?"

"Visiting my favorite author."

I looked at him intently. "Seriously. What are you doing in New York?"

A laugh escaped him as he nodded. "Visiting my favorite author. Just like I said."

"How did you know I was here tonight?"

"Your website." He narrowed his eyes. "Your newsletter. Your blog posts. Perhaps a few of your social media posts. Now I sound like a stalker."

"To some extent, yes." I laughed lightly.

"I've been wanting to see you at one of your events, but it never seemed to work out. I made up my mind a few days ago that I was coming here to see you this weekend no matter what. So, I dropped everything and booked a flight."

"What about Phil? What if he decided to come with me on this trip?"

"I wanted to take my chances."

"I see."

"He's not with you, I assume."

I shook my head. "He had things back home. It's nice when he comes, but he has his own career, too."

"So, where are you headed?"

"Home," I replied.

"Oh. I didn't know you lived here."

"Well, not full time. Just occasionally. The hotel fees were getting as high as apartment rental costs due to the many events here. So, I've been renting a condo a few blocks from this bookstore for the last, gosh, fourteen years now."

"I'm happy things have been going well for you. You deserve it."

"Thank you. I'm very grateful for being able to have this as my career."

"Can I at least see you safely to your door?"

"I would love that."

Chapter 3

Isabel

The sound of the binder crashing to the floor and the sun's rays on my face woke me up. I picked up the binder, put it on the coffee table, and then laid back down to gaze at the ceiling. The absence of sirens, honking horns, and traffic noise made for a strange morning wake-up. In the distance, I could hear the faint sound of a phone ringing. I realized it was my cellphone and hurried from the couch to the kitchen table, where my bag was placed the previous night.

"Charlize? Charlize?" I said as I fumbled to answer the phone.

"Isabel? How are you?"

"Oh, good. I didn't miss your call."

"Everything okay?"

"Everything is fantastic. I was going to call you last night before I went to bed, but I ended up passed out on the couch. I just woke up a few minutes ago."

"Really?" She laughed. "Isabel, it's almost nine in the morning."

"Obviously I was tired." I laughed as I stretched.

"So, how is the cabin?"

"Dreamy. Romantic. Cozy. I could live here forever and write. I can see why Zetta never wanted to leave."

"Sounds nice. You'll have to send me some pics. Did you get all settled?"

"Last night, yes. Today, I'm going to head into town and grab some coffee. Then come back and finish reading what I was reading before I fell asleep last night."

"Well, I didn't hear from you, so I wanted to check in and make sure everything was okay. Let me know if you need anything. I shipped out a printer and some reams of paper, along with extra ink. That should arrive sometime this week, I'd assume."

"Thank you!"

"I know this is a big project you're undertaking. So reach out anytime, okay?"

"I will. Thank you."

"Well, you have a good day. Enjoy your coffee and send me that first chapter once you have it outlined."

"Will do. Thank you, Charlize."

Just as my phone warned me about its seven percent battery, I ended the call. I rummaged through my bag for the cord and power adapter and plugged it into the outlet under the table.

I was not accustomed to such silence. Despite the discomfort, I adored it. It felt like I was on vacation. In a way, I was. A working vacation. As I looked around the room I hoped this job would change my life; or, at a minimum, advance my career. I'd been in the same position for years, and a new role would be exciting.

"*Take a left out of the driveway and that will lead you straight into town,*" I recalled Iris explaining. "*Straight shot. It's impossible for you to lose your way.*"

The trip into town was beautiful. The changing leaves indicated fall was approaching. I felt a sense of excitement being in the Northwoods during autumn. It already didn't compare to the photos I'd seen online or on calendars.

Being unfamiliar with the area, I drove with caution. I was focused on the road edges to avoid hitting any animals that could dart out.

With a loud roar, a massive truck sped up and changed lanes to pass. I shook my head as the rusted and faded Chevy truck sped on ahead.

Once I arrived in town, I followed the signs that led to Main Street. I parked my car after a few blocks and saw the coffee shop right in front of me.

I lucked out in my parking spot, laughing out loud at the happenstance.

Upon entering the coffee shop, I was struck by the intense scent of coffee so strong that it was almost tangible.

"Can I help you?"

"Yes," I smiled as I approached the counter. "I'll take a large, iced turtle mocha with white chocolate. And can I have that with oat milk?"

I watched the cashier hit some buttons on the till before turning her gaze back to me. "Oat milk. Anything else? Muffins? Donuts? A fresh dozen just came out of the oven."

"What kind of muffins do you have this morning?"

"Raisin. Oatmeal. Blueberry. Lemon poppy seed. And strudel."

"Lemon poppy seed, please."

"Anything else?"

"No. I think that will do it," I replied as I handed her my card.

As the door opened, I looked over at the man entering. Before waving to the cashier, he nodded and smiled at me.

"Good morning, Em!" He smiled.

"Morning, Evan. You up here for the weekend?"

"I am," he answered. "A lot of work to get done before that snow flies, you know."

"Oh, don't we know?" She laughed. "I've been caught off guard and snowed in too many times. Would you like your usual?"

"Please," he said as he made his way to the bulletin board covered in fliers and business cards.

"Here's your card back, and it'll be just a minute or two."

I thanked her with a smile, then moved aside to examine the assortment of baked goods.

"Probably don't need these on the board anymore, huh?" Evan asked as he slid the cashier some business cards.

"No. Probably not. Unless she's going to write books from her grave."

"What a sad woman. Must've been a lonely life in that cabin all alone all those years."

I acted preoccupied with putting my credit card away, all the while listening to their conversation.

"You know, I did hear there's a woman staying there in her cabin. Going to write her life story or something like that," Em stated. "Don't quote me. Just something I heard."

"Really."

"Yeah."

"Just what we need. Before you know it, they'll have a sign up and dedicate the god damn town to Zetta Castellan."

Em acknowledged with a nod while placing a paper bag on the display case.

"Here's your coffee, ma'am. And your fresh baked muffin."

"Thank you very much," I replied as I pretended to look for something in my purse.

"You have to admit, Evan, her books sold well. You don't become a household name by doing something mediocre."

"My opinion is she made a mistake by bringing her past to this town. She should've left it where it was. If you want my take, she was attempting to escape her problems. She likely discovered too late that the issue was with herself, not what she believed she was escaping."

"Live and learn," Em replied as I grabbed my coffee and muffin.

"Thank you." I nodded at both of them.

"Have a good day," Em said as I walked out of the shop.

Now, Zetta's story had me even more intrigued.

What problems? What was the thing she was trying to get away from? Who was Evan, and why the negative attitude towards Zetta? What else did he know? How did they know about me when I had only just become familiar with this project? In small towns news traveled fast, without a doubt.

I settled into my car, and as I turned it on I caught sight of a nearby vehicle. It looked like the faded blue truck that passed me on the way into town.

Chapter 4

Zetta

I placed my writing bag on my desk and smiled when Phil walked into my office. The journey home to Wisconsin had gone without a hitch, and it felt nice to be back.

"Well, how was your signing?" he asked as we hugged.

"It went very well."

"I'm glad you're home. We all missed you."

"We all, huh?"

"Oh, come on, Zetta. Do we have to start this right off the bat?"

"I'm sorry. I know you missed me. I feel that."

Silence took hold of the moment, and although I knew I should've kept quiet when he made that comment I didn't. I had a habit of involving my feelings and ruining good moments. I let out a long breath and leaned against him, resting my head on his shoulder.

"I'm sorry. It's been a long weekend."

"I'll let you unpack," he said as he kissed the top of my head. Before he closed the door behind him, he turned to me. "We're having bacon chicken pasta and Caesar salad for dinner if you'd like to join us as a family."

He closed the door, and I wondered what other blended families also felt like their life was constantly going through a blender. With a sigh, I plugged in my laptop and settled into my chair. No motivational meditations were strong enough to drag me out from under this life. I wanted out, but I also wanted to stay. Despite his inability to recognize the signs or hear my pleas, I still loved him. After all, he didn't put us in this situation.

This was a new territory for both of us. In his mind, ignoring the problems was the solution to make them disappear. Only, they didn't disappear. Our demise was carried out with meticulousness.

I needed time to prepare. With every tick of the clock, I grew more certain that I was getting closer to walking out that door forever. The other issue was that I had no idea how to stay strong enough to leave.

I pulled my phone from my bag and checked for missed calls. There were none. However, I had a text from Catherine that she and her fiancé had safely arrived back home. After replying, I placed my bag under my desk and put my phone in my pocket before heading down the stairs for dinner.

I wasn't hungry, and just wanted to take a hot bath and head to bed. Nevertheless, I realized that skipping dinner would be used against me in the long run. The dreadful sensation in my chest grew with each step I took. Deep breathing, fake smiling, and counting to ten didn't do much to relieve the tension. When I entered the room, I was greeted in the usual manner.

With silence.

Phil had his back turned and was cooking something on the stove. A few of the girls shifted their attention towards the door before resuming their conversations. No acknowledgement was given. There wasn't even a hint of a smile or nod, or a welcome home. Nothing.

"Dinner smells good, babe," I said as I stood next to him. My hand rested on his lower back.

"Can you grab a potholder?"

I nodded, opened the drawer and pulled out a potholder, setting it on the island next to all the other dinner dishes.

My phone rang as I closed the drawer.

"Who's that?" Phil asked while carrying the pot from the stove to the island and setting it on the potholder.

I pulled the phone from my pocket and my heart stopped.

"Work," I barely managed to say.

"Who?"

"Work. Catherine. I should take this," I said as I answered the phone and stepped into the foyer.

"Hello?"

"Did you make it home okay?"

"You can't be calling me like this!" I whispered as I glanced back towards the kitchen.

Although I knew I shouldn't have given Jed my cell number, I went against what I felt. The texts we sent back and forth before I got home made me feel noticed and valued. For the first time in years

I didn't feel invisible, like a burden, or just existing and begging to be noticed.

"I just wanted to make sure you made it home. You didn't respond to my texts."

"I haven't read anything yet. I'm making dinner."

"I miss you, Zetta. I had a good time. And I hope you did, too. I can't stop thinking about you. About us, and—"

"I need to go."

"I want to see you again."

"We'll talk again later. Thank you." I hung up and placed the phone back in my pocket.

"Everything okay?" Phil asked when I returned to the kitchen.

I nodded as I turned on the faucet to wash my hands.

"Yes. We just forgot a few things at the bookstore. I'll pick them up when I get over that way again. Good thing it's nothing important."

"Dinner is ready, girls," Phil sang as he turned to smile at them.

I leaned against the sink drying my hands and watched as all five girls huddled around the island to fill their plates with pasta and salad. They all enjoyed a casual conversation, and I felt like the third wheel or some fly on the wall, observing what should be a wonderful family moment. Phil made some jokes, and the girls laughed as they took their plates over to the dining room table.

"You going to eat?" he asked as he glanced over at me.

I nodded as I placed the towel next to the sink. I grabbed a plate and dished up some salad, trying to think of anything and everything I could to prevent myself from breaking down into tears. The previous seven years had been a complete nightmare, and unfortunately the eighth year was proving to be even worse. I'd become an outcast within my own family. A doormat. Invisible to everyone. I was ignored when I tried to communicate. My tears went unnoticed by everyone. However, in public, everyone exchanged masks and we became a united and joyful family. I've never witnessed such impressive manipulation skills in children.

I thought back to Jed Conley's arms around me, and the warmth of him made me smile. The lump in my throat diminished, but the sensation of his touch on my skin and the taste of him on my lips persisted. He had a knack for saying exactly what needed to be said. The impact of his words was much greater than his familiar empty promises. At this point, I pondered which was the worse of the two: living with a family that made you feel like an invisible autoimmune disorder, or being embraced by another man who made you forget your true numbness.

Chapter 5

Isabel

I walked down the hallway to Zetta's room and placed my hand on the knob. Entering her bedroom felt awkward. However, like the rest of the cabin, her room was cozy.

The room had a lower vaulted ceiling crisscrossed with beautiful wood beams. Sheer curtains hung from the ridge beam, reaching the walls. The open spaces between the curtains were illuminated by string lights.

A half-wall wooden bookshelf stood against the far wall, just under the big bay window. The headboard of Zetta's bed was placed against the wall next to it. Positioned on each side of her bed were wooden nightstands, crowned with a mirror in the shape of an oval that extended from the stand to the ceiling.

Two rows of pillows decorated her bed, and extra cashmere blankets were placed on the comforter. The bed looked luxurious.

To the right was a double door which led to a walk-in closet. The closet was divided, with clothing and shoes on the right side and shelving with wicker baskets of different sizes on the left side. In the middle of the far wall there was a makeup station featuring a mirror bordered by bulb lights.

I loved the rustic look and feel of her entire cabin, and now, seeing her bedroom, I could tell she had a knack for making things feel luxurious, cozy, and welcoming. A part of me wanted to stay here forever.

But my home was in New York. Everything that mattered to me—including my family, friends, and countless memories—was in the city. I couldn't see myself living anywhere other than the city. However, this rustic cabin took second place as a vacation spot I'd love to go to.

I ran my fingers over her garments while heading towards her makeup area. I switched on the lights and took out the chair. While gazing at my reflection, I questioned what it would be like to see Zetta getting ready. Based on the glass bottles on her tabletop, my guess is that she invested in the most opulent skincare brand on the market. I glanced into her drawer and found multiple tubes of maroon mascara along with various light shades of lip gloss.

I picked up a tube of lip gloss and read the bottom. Nude.

I applied it to my lower lip and pressed my lips together. It had a glossy appearance and a subtle color.

I grabbed a pink bottle of perfume. Flowerbomb.

As I removed the cap, I delighted in the beautiful blend of floral and vanilla notes—the most captivating aroma of a perfume I had ever come across. Since there were no other perfume bottles, I presumed Zetta used this one as her signature scent.

I glanced at the wall of wicker baskets, and a partially hidden book caught my attention. What an odd place for a book. A part of it was concealed by a basket. After another brief inspection, it was the only basket that was not perfectly lined up on the shelf.

I stood up, grabbed the book, and flipped it open.

Zetta's handwritten words left me in shock as I slid down to the floor. I was intrigued by the brief section of the manuscript I'd read last night. Yet the words she wrote in this journal felt like a sudden blow to my stomach.

The date was January 1st, 1998.

Just as I flipped the page the doorbell rang, causing me to jump. It was followed by a few forceful knocks.

I emerged from the closet, placed her journal on her bed, and left the room.

I let out a sigh of relief when I saw the delivery truck in the driveway as I walked towards the door. My printer had arrived, just as Charlize said it would.

"Isabel Vinson?"

I acknowledged by nodding.

"Just need you to sign here."

I used my finger to create my signature on his handheld device screen.

"Thanks," he said as he stepped towards his truck and grabbed a box. "Where would you like these? One is pretty heavy."

"Um, how about right here on the porch," I suggested as I propped open the door.

He set the first box in the doorway, and I shifted it aside.

"This is a nice place you have," he said while bringing in the second box.

"Oh, it's not mine. I'm just visiting."

"Oh," he said as he studied me. "Well, whoever owns this, tell them it looks nice. It's rare to find cabins around here that are as nice-looking as this one. It's good to see a nice place, and one so well cared for."

I nodded.

After he left, I closed the door and stared at the boxes. First, I had to decide where to place the printer and then figure out how to connect it to my laptop. The task seemed daunting, and I opted instead to read more of Zetta's journal.

Just as I was about to enter, something in my peripheral vision grabbed my attention.

I stared at the house next door and noticed a bonfire. Shortly after, a man emerged from the woods and placed brush onto the fire.

Chapter 6

Zetta

New Years Day 1998

I don't know why I stay in this marriage. I question my reasons for staying in a family that has no interest in me. Last night was awful. Phil and I attended a New Year's Eve celebration. What was supposed to be a good time was spitefully ruined.

Women from town made their whispers obvious for a good majority of the party. I stayed with Phil for a bit, then ventured outside for some fresh air. Even after sharing the women's words with Phil, I was advised to ignore it.

You can only ignore for so long. And it hurt. Phil's supposed 'respectful' behavior of being nice and cordial felt like a backstab. I knew something like this was going to happen tonight. The women in this town had a reputation for being two-faced and gossip-loving. They made a habit of maliciously meddling in others' lives while concealing their own secrets, and it took a lot of practice to make it appear flawless.

While I was outside, I heard a door close. A man

walked out, lit a cigarette, and stood behind me. The smell of the cigarette mixed with his cologne was an unrecognizable yet intriguing scent, to say the least.

* * * * *

"Need an escape from inside there, too, huh?"

I turned to gaze up at him. "More than you know."

"Who you here with? I'm Jed, by the way. Jed Conley. Don't get up," he said as I made a move to stand. "I'll come sit by you. You don't bite, do you?" Making his way around the stone wall, he settled down beside me.

I grinned. "The response will differ depending on the person you ask."

"It usually does," he laughed. "Want some?" He offered me his cigarette when he sat down beside me.

"I don't smoke."

"I didn't think so. Just wanted to ask. You okay if I smoke? Or, I can put it out and—"

"It's fine. The smoke from your cigarette won't be what kills me."

"Lighten up," he replied. "It's a new year. I'm sure you have some resolutions you're starting. Or some new trends to try, like all the other women these days."

"If you call starting a new life a trend, then I guess—"

"Uh-oh." He stared at me as he inhaled deeply. "It seems like something is not going as planned. So, what's your name?"

"Zetta."

"Do you have a last name?"

"Castellan."

"As in Phil Castellan—"

I laughed and nodded. "Guilty."

"He seems like a nice guy."

"He is a nice man. Surprisingly, the issues are not with him. Well, not completely him. He's not to blame, but he's not taking any initiative." I hesitated. "Never mind. I shouldn't have said anything. It was nice to meet you, Jed Conley," I said as I stood. "I wish you a good New Year."

"Oh, wait. Zetta." He stood and followed me. "Zetta, wait. If I said something wrong, I didn't mean to. I was just—"

"It's okay."

"No. It's not okay. C'mon. Stop."

I paused long enough to keep the tears inside.

"I'm not one of them, if it makes you feel any better," he said as he gestured towards the house with a nod. "I'm just here to be seen for a few minutes and then sneak off into the night. I hate these events anyway. They're not really my thing."

"I'd better get inside."

"You know what? Hold on." He stared at me. "Please, just wait here. I'll be right back."

I took a deep breath, nodded, and watched him disappear into the house. I tried to stop the tears by diverting my attention to amusing thoughts. It only made me feel worse at that moment. A few minutes later, Jed came walking out of the house.

"Put this in your pocket," he said as he handed me a piece of paper.

"What is it?"

"My number."

"Why would I need your phone number, Jed Conley?" I laughed as I handed the paper back to him. "I can't take this."

He put his hands in the air and shook his head. "In case you need me."

"And just what would I need you for?"

"Hey. I may not know your entire story, but it's clear that you're not happy and something is really upsetting you. If you're happy, then great! Fantastic. Toss it away. Shred it, or burn it if that's what you want to do. If you never need to call me, then all is well. But if for some reason you find yourself in a situation that you need someone, you call me."

I shook my head and stared at him.

"Hey. I give you my word. I will always be there for you."

"You don't even know me."

"You're right. I don't know you. But I will say that you're the most gorgeous woman here at this party. And there's a certain vibe about you that's different. I like it. And if I was Phil Castellan, I wouldn't let you out of my sight. If I didn't know any better, I'd say he's losing you. It's written all over your face. I can hear it in your voice. Keep it in case you need it." He nodded to my hand that was holding his handwritten number.

* * * * * * *

"And what, Zetta? What?" Phil yelled as he paced our bedroom floor. "Just to clarify, you're suggesting that I should have left the party because you were concerned about women discussing you in a negative way? This is ridiculous. Are you aware of how immature this all appears?"

"That's not what I'm saying. I told you what they said. I overheard your conversation with them and watched you act like it was no big deal. That what they were doing was okay!" Tears streamed down my face as I sat on the bed, trying to catch my breath.

"You know, maybe the kids are right. Maybe the issue lies in how you're treating them, not with them."

"How dare you!" I spat at him.

"What?" He paused and threw his hands in the air. "What? You're the adult. They're kids, Zetta. Kids!" And just like that, he twisted the events of this evening around to point more fingers at me.

"And kids can be very hurtful!" I blurted. I knew better than to engage on a topic that had nothing to do with this evening. It was a regular tactic of Phil's. But I played right into it again.

"Everyone is hurtful to you. Tell me one person who treats you well. You think everyone treats you horribly. It seems like you're always the one who gets victimized."

"I've been telling you for years, Phil, what your daughters have been doing and saying. Years! You blow it off and do nothing. You let it go, and you know it's only teaching them it's okay to treat me like that. All you're doing is encouraging their behavior towards me. And the only thing it's going to do is teach them how to be master manipulators when they're adults."

"You know, I think I'll be sleeping in my office

tonight. What a great way to celebrate the New Year. Thank you, Zetta. Thank you for a wonderful New Year! Cheers to us!"

I held my breath as he stormed from the room, slamming the door behind him.

I sat on the bed and cried, wondering where my marriage had gone wrong. I found it unbelievable how something so beautiful could be destroyed, and no one else seemed to see it except me. The tears dried up when I understood the lack of value I had in this family. They all accused me as if I was the one who started it all. I wish I had been the one to light the match. At least then I might feel something. Right now, I felt nothing. Completely numb. We had no control over everything that was happening. But I guess every blended family needs a scapegoat. There was no one more fitting than me to take on that title. I was willing to be the villain or the scapegoat. I'd be whatever I need to be to get out of this family.

The door opened, and Phil walked in to toss some duffle bags onto the floor.

"What's that for?"

"In case you want to leave again. Feel free. I have more bags I can bring up from the basement." And with that he walked from the room, slamming the door behind him for a second time.

Chapter 7

Isabel

I sat at the table and opened my laptop. Why was I so upset over a past that didn't belong to me? I was heated and angry, and every piece of me wanted to rush to Zetta's defense. Since time travel was impossible, I wrote down notes for her story. A story I was about to tell. Her side of the story.

I flipped open her binder, and I knew I had one puzzle piece amongst the many others sitting on her bookshelves. I re-read her checklist for the autobiography.

Tell the story from my perspective.

Get lost in the depths of my life.

Give my music a listen.

Read the books on my shelves.

Wear my perfume, clothing, and shoes, if they fit.

Experience my life firsthand and understand the person I used to be.

Judge me based on your own perception of me, not influenced by others.

I glanced outside after reading her notes. I got a longing sense that she felt alone most of the time.

Some of it might be related to what I caught Evan saying in the coffee shop. In recounting her story, I had to remain vigilant and prevent others from planting ideas in my mind that distorted Zetta's identity. I was the only other person who had an insight into her true identity. Oh, and Iris too. I was curious about how much Iris truly knew about her.

I went back to typing out as much as I could recall from what I'd read so far. I intended to label each journal with a post-it note and assign a unique log number to make it easier to reference, beginning with the binder and the journal I left on her bed.

The journal from her closet dated back to 1998, which seemed like a good starting place. A quarter of a century has passed. The best scenario would be if I could find and read the corresponding journals in the correct order. I was curious about why that particular journal was in the closet instead of on the bookshelves. Was its intended place supposed to be hidden? Tucked away and not easily seen? Was I not supposed to find this one yet? Did Zetta somehow guide me to her closet and the journal that started her story?

Maybe another individual tried to hide the inception and how everything began. Nothing was out of order in Zetta's perfectly kept home. This journal was the first thing I noticed that was not orderly. Predictably, my imagination conjured up a multitude of situations that could have unfolded.

I started typing a timeline on a separate document for easier tracking. I hadn't yet settled on the starting point, but having a timeline would allow me to map out the events and find the perfect location.

I heard a high-pitched noise and glanced out the window. Since the house right next door was the closest one for miles, it had to be where the noise was coming from. I wrote down some additional notes before getting up to close the porch door and reduce the noise.

I glanced at the neighbor's and saw the man from earlier leaf blowing the yard. I stepped to the side of the window and watched as he blew all the leaves past the fire pit and into the woods. It puzzled me why he chose to spend time blowing leaves while residing in the middle of the woods.

His fire was still burning strong, and I could see that he had cleaned up his side of the iron fence. I was curious about who was responsible for maintaining Zetta's yard, or if I had to do it as well. I couldn't remember having seen that specific clause in the contract before I signed it. I also had no idea who was to mow the yard. And if it snowed while I was here, who was responsible for plowing the driveway? I made a mental note to get a hold of Iris for clarification.

I kept my eyes on the man next door as I went from window to window to keep sight of what he was doing. From a distance, he looked to be around my age. Although I'd never been good at guessing ages. So he could have been a few years younger or older. People thought I look very young for my age. It was common for me to be mistaken for a teenager, even though I was in my mid-twenties. I supposed I could view that as a positive, considering I'd appear youthful in my forties. Well, as long as I kept up with good skincare.

I recalled my mother telling me how important it was to wash all my makeup off each night and moisturize, moisturize, moisturize. Drink lots of water and never leave the house without sunscreen. My mother looked very well put together and was gorgeous at her age. Despite not being able to compare my physical traits to hers because of being adopted, I was determined to maintain the same routine she has followed her whole life. Whether you inherited good genes or not, your skin's health was influenced by what you put inside and on your body.

I walked into Zetta's kitchen and looked in her fridge.

Raw veggies, fresh fruits, and greens. It seemed like Zetta was also mindful of her nutrition.

In looking at her recent photos, I noticed that her long silver hair was peppered with some black. Her signature look for photographs included a low ponytail and a black turtleneck. Her appearance was both elegant and casually simple. I felt a ping of sadness that she only lived fifty-three years.

I needed to know what happened from 1998 until her death in 2023. Did her divorce from Phil make her a lonely woman all these years, like Evan from the coffee shop assumed? I couldn't imagine a woman as gorgeous as her staying single. Then again, there were instances where being single resulted in more joy in life. Especially if you'd already done the marriage path, and it didn't work out. Regardless, she made an excellent name for herself. And from the outside looking in, I'd say she lived a wonderful life.

Again, there could be a veil shrouding the truth

around her life.

Chapter 8

Zetta

As I entered the house, I placed my keys on the counter while Jed followed behind me. This property had been on the market for three months. When the realtor showed it to me, I knew it was perfect. It was far enough away from the negative memories of my hometown. Although it was out in the woods and there were no neighbors, the town was welcoming and small. And no one knew me. It was a new beginning and just the thing I needed.

"This place is very nice," Jed said as he toured the main level. "With a few updates, you can have this place feeling homey."

I nodded as I watched him.

Life had been crazy and stressful for the past two months. Between packing up my belongings, moving house and filing for divorce, I was exhausted. I wanted a place to call my own, a place to relax in and not have to worry about walking on eggshells.

"Well, what do you say we consummate the—"

"Stop." I tapped him on the arm as he reached for me.

"What?"

I shook my head. "There's more to see. I want to show you the real reason I bought this place."

"The real reason?" he questioned as he followed me out of the house, down the porch, and through the backyard.

There was a row of dead pine trees with a small opening that I ventured through.

"Where are we going?"

"Look!" I beamed as we stood on the other side of the trees.

"A shed?"

"Well, not just a shed. Imagine it as a cabin, but on a smaller scale. It already has a bedroom and a tiny bathroom. Because of their small size, the living area and kitchen are combined into one. And look at the front porch! Oh, I love it!"

"Zetta," he said as he studied me. "This place looks like it's been sitting vacant for too long, and I don't think I'd like you staying in this place. The house, yes. But not—"

"Hear me out."

"Hearing." He smiled.

"This run-down cabin is going to be my office or writing studio. I'm going to fix it up. I've been searching for design photos for weeks and I know how I want it to look. I can keep all my writing in here. All my books. And when I'm done writing, I can walk back home. It's going to be perfect."

He smiled as stared at me. "I love it. It's a great idea."

"Thank you." I smiled at him. "The house is already livable, so I want to get started on this place right away."

"I'd love to help."

I stared at him.

"Please. I can turn this place into your dream studio. Let me do it."

"You sure?"

"More than anything. You deserve this. You just show me your pictures and I'll get to work, and we'll have you in here writing more books in no time."

I ran into his arms and kissed him. If I'd learned anything over the last few years, it was that love shouldn't hurt.

I hadn't been this happy in years. It had been so long since my smile felt genuine; since I'd spoken my true feelings and someone was there to listen and not tell me my feelings were unjustified, or a fallout from overthinking.

It took me weeks to make up my mind about calling Jed. I hit rock bottom and, despite begging for help and spending days in tears, I was unnoticed—especially by my family. Those best friends who say they'll be there through hell or high water must've drowned somewhere along the way.

I found myself alone. Scared. Numb. And not knowing if life was worth staying for. The woman in the mirror was someone I'd never seen before. Just an empty shell. There was nothing left to feel. Nothing left to say. I had reached my breaking point, and I was ready to call it quits.

My marriage was over. I was celebrating my career milestones and accomplishments privately, as my professional life was thriving. No one stood by my side. As I desperately sought a shoulder to lean on, no one sat next to me. Since no one saw, no one understood.

When I screamed, nobody took me seriously. I was the one who appeared irrational for leaving behind a perfectly good marriage and wonderful family. At this point, I was the person who destroyed a once-good life. I remained quiet about the situation at home to uphold a specific image. Our family was trapped in a picture-perfect concept. Once inside, each person settled into their respective roles.

However, there was an abundance of secrets and lies. Pictures of fake smiles and heavenly bliss were used to decorate the walls. The perfect husband and the perfect wife. People rejected the truth but eagerly indulged in gossip. Despite the closed doors, everyone somehow knew what had occurred and witnessed the crumbling of the charming facade.

At some point, they'd discover who was responsible for lighting that match. The truth would come out when the time was right. And then it would make complete sense why I decided to walk away from a flawless marriage and the perfect family. Or why I never defended myself and just left town.

Short truth is it was never my battle to fight.

"You okay?"

I gazed up at Jed and nodded.

"Yes." I smiled. "Everything is perfect. Well, everything is *going* to be absolutely perfect."

"Everything is already perfect." He grinned. "You have to believe that. Speak it. Live it. Your life is already perfect."

"There's a reason why I keep you around."

"Oh, I see!" He laughed as he turned to face the

cabin. "Your life is perfect. Take photos now of this place. Lots of them. This is your story in real life. They had the power to knock you down and you lost your footing. You feel like this cabin. Desolate. Empty. Ugly. Invisible. No one has cared about you in years. But you still have life yet. You're building something more than just this cabin, Zetta. You don't have to tell me. I know what you're capable of, and you're about to take on the world."

I smiled up at him.

"And I'll be right here with you," he continued.

"Holding my hand," I said.

He nodded and smiled. "I'll never let you go, Zetta."

Chapter 9

Isabel

A week had passed. I opened the cupboard, realizing the dire need to head into town for groceries. I had been living off of ramen and canned soups, and barely slept or moved myself from the kitchen table.

My life had been completely taken over by the stack of journals, now marked and labeled for quick reference. Her journals made me laugh and cry at different moments, reminding me of the loneliness she endured throughout her life.

Her awards, release parties, and tours were concealed within this cabin, as if they were a tightly kept secret. Strangers from different countries celebrated her secret and showed their appreciation by sending cards, letters, and gifts. The trinkets and decorations suddenly made sense. A significant portion of it consisted of gifts given by her readers. She took the time to write thank-you notes to each person and made a note of it.

I made the kitchen area my temporary office space. In Zetta's shed, I came across a folding table which I repurposed to hold the printer, toner, and paper reams.

I was in a productive flow, completely absorbed in my reading, note-taking, and writing, and didn't want to disrupt it by going to town.

I gathered my hair into a low ponytail and checked my reflection in the mirror. Sleeping in Zetta's bed this past week was like sleeping on the most luxurious mattress you could imagine. Even with just a few hours of sleep, I felt rejuvenated and motivated to work on her story.

Slipping into her black boots, I gave myself one more look in the mirror. Black leggings, a black turtleneck, small gold hoop earrings, and a beige vest. I grabbed a beige clutch from her closet and swapped my items into it before leaving the room. At first glance at her closet, it seemed like she had a diverse collection of clothes. It wasn't until I closely examined her clothes that I noticed the presence of three distinct colors. Her primary colors consisted of black and ivory. In addition, she owned scarves, gloves, and belts in maroon. Deciding what to wear each morning was easy, and never time- consuming. I had spent the last few days immersing myself deeper into her life by dressing in her clothing, which fit me perfectly, and enjoying some of her favorite foods throughout the day.

I walked out of the cabin and towards my car, the scent of rain filling the warm fall morning. The morning weather forecast showed thunderstorms later in the day. While I enjoyed thunderstorms, I had mixed feelings about being alone in the cabin during a severe one. With no basement in the cabin,

I couldn't help but think about the possibility of a tornado.

"Hey!"

I pressed the button to unlock my car.

"Hey! Good morning over there!"

I paused and looked around before realizing it was the man from the house next door. Surprised, I maintained my gaze until he broke the silence and greeted me again.

"Um, hi," I replied as I glanced around.

"I didn't mean to scare you, but I wanted to say hi. I'm Weston. I didn't know for sure if anyone was staying here. Usually it's empty when I'm up here. Well, since she passed and all." He pointed to Zetta's cabin.

"I'm Isabel." I smiled. "I'm just staying here for a few weeks. Working on a project and was looking for a quiet place to stay. And, well, here I am." I didn't feel comfortable explaining the real reason for my stay to a stranger.

"Well, nice to meet you, Isabel." He extended his hand and I reached for it.

"And nice to meet you."

"I hope I'm not causing too much noise. There's just a lot of cleanup, and winter is coming soon. Sometimes it arrives in September. But usually it's more like October. The last thing I want to do is work in the yard when it's cold."

"You live here? There?" I asked as I pointed to the house on the other side of the fence.

"No." He shook his head. "Not yet. I'd love to own this place. The man who owned this place was as close to a dad as I'll ever get. He passed away a couple of years ago, and left it to me in his will. But the legal process, you know how that can go. So I'm just maintaining the place until I get the go-ahead to sign the papers and move in."

I nodded. "Well, that was nice of him. Sorry to hear he passed."

Weston nodded slowly. "He's the only one who was ever there for me. It's hard without him, I'll admit that. Some days are brutal and... I'm sorry." He paused. "I'm sorry. You don't want to hear all that."

"It's all good," I replied. "I'm sorry for your loss."

"I just wanted to say hi, and if I'm too loud please feel free to come and tell me, or yell across the yard at me." He smiled. "I won't take offense to it. I'm used to being alone up here and making all the noise I want. But I'll try to keep it down over there."

"Well, it's nice to meet you, Weston. I hope it all works out and you get to move in soon."

"Well, I'll let you get back to your errands or whatever you were doing. Nice meeting you, Isabel."

I got into my car and watched him walk back to the house. I read in one of Zetta's journals that she was no longer staying in the house. She loved the cabin too much and couldn't see herself staying in the house. The person she sold it to is still a mystery to me.

I drove into town and stopped at the coffee shop before hitting the grocery store. I parked in front of the shop and walked inside. At a corner table, three women stared at me and exchanged hushed whispers. I received a brief nod and a smile from only one of them.

"Can I help you?"

"Yes. Um, one large iced turtle mocha—"

"With oat milk," Em finished, smiling at me. "I remember you. You came back."

I smiled and nodded. "I did."

"Would you like another lemon poppy seed muffin as well?"

"That would be fabulous." I grinned at her. "Thank you so much for remembering."

"Don't pay any attention to them," she whispered as I handed her my card.

"Uh, who?"

"Most rumors in town can be traced back to one of those three individuals."

"Oh!" I nodded when I realized she was talking about the table where the three women were.

"Say, can I ask you a question?"

"Sure," she replied.

"Last time I was in here, there was a man."

"Evan," she told me, then laughed. "Yes. Don't pay any attention to him, either. Some people think they know everything about everyone's business. I just let it slide. Not my place to judge."

"Okay. He just mentioned Zetta Castellan and—"

"Oh, that part." Em nodded as she pursed her lips. "Yeah. She moved here, and I'm not sure of all the details about her move. I've heard a lot of different things about that. But I believe they knew each other. A little more than friends, if you know what I mean."

Shocked, I held my breath as she gave me back my card.

More than friends?

Another puzzle piece fit, shedding light on his

negativity towards Zetta. If she was in a relationship with him and broke things off with him, this would all make sense.

I quickly glanced around the coffee shop and caught all three women stealing glances at me before returning their attention to one another. I turned to watch Em make my coffee and smiled. It was surprising to see a bunch of adult women acting like a clique of teenage girls.

It wasn't until I got back to the cabin that I realized all the stares from the visit into town could very well have been because I was dressed in Zetta's clothes. Handbag and all.

Chapter 10

Zetta

The last month was nothing short of an amazing summer. Once Jed finished my cabin, I fell in love with it and opted to stay there while he was away back home. It was the perfect size for just me, and turned out better than I could've imagined.

Phil suggested that we discuss matters. I have to be honest there is really nothing to discuss, but I can empathize with him. It's not until something is gone that you realize its worth. It's sad it took my leaving for Phil to see what was happening in our home. And now that he sees, and is defending not only himself but me as well, it's creating a tension like no other in that town.

People are torn about what side to take. Who to believe. What to believe. Everyone seems fixated on how I ruined a good thing. Sometimes you can't win. And this is one hill I don't care to die on.

Our divorce hearing is coming up, and it's coming at a good time. Since I left my life has been coming back together, and I'm really happy. The sales of my books are going strong, and my publisher has already planned tours and talk show appearances for next year. It's true that when one door closes ten more open up.

On top of that, Jed and I have been doing okay with this relationship. The distance has been a challenge at times, but I understand that his job is located back home and there are no well-paying jobs in this area.

I've been doing everything I can to avoid the constant emails and voicemails from women in my hometown, especially one. One thing I've learned about some of those women is that you can't trust them. You just can't. Yes, I've moved on and am doing well. My life is wonderful, and Jed and I are looking forward to a future together. And there are some people who just can't handle that and need to meddle in your life.

I've been searching for a job for Jed over this way. Sometimes things happen for a reason. Planned or unplanned. Three days ago, I found out that we're expecting. I've been trying to think of a way to surprise him, as we've talked about starting a family. I just didn't think it was going to happen right away.

I'm experiencing a blend of fear and excitement simultaneously. I've kept the news to myself. Given how public my life is becoming, I think it's best to keep this between Jed and me. I'm also concerned about balancing my growing career and having a newborn. I'm worried that my agent and publisher will have to reschedule or cancel some of the upcoming events.

Maybe I'm not meant to go on tour. Maybe starting a family and writing as a hobby is the direction I should head towards. Either scenario leads to a positive outcome. The right time is when everything falls into place. Jed and I are both ready for this.

I bought a dozen roses and some non-alcoholic wine to celebrate tonight. I'm planning on surprising Jed. I've already packed for the weekend and just hope he doesn't call while I'm on the way. I ordered a dad-to-be shirt for him from an online store and wrote a lengthy letter detailing my love for him and my excitement for our future as a family.

Chapter 11

Isabel

I arranged all the journals on the table and began skimming through the unread ones. I was experiencing a range of emotions. Then my phone rang.

"Hey, Isabel!" Charlize greeted. "How are things?"

"Good."

"You okay? You sound off."

"Charlize, I'm fine, but... I need to gather myself," I said, pausing and taking a deep breath before sitting down.

"Isabel, what's going on?"

"Charlize, something isn't right."

"What do you mean? What happened?"

"I'm taking notes on everything. Scanning documents I need. I have my timeline, which looks like a mess, but it's really an organized mess. I'm angry. Confused. And..."

"Angry at who?"

"Do you know anything about this job? This woman Zetta?" I asked.

"I'm sorry. I was just contacted by upper management and told that you were heading out there on this assignment. What happened?"

"I thought this would be an easy job. Read her journals. Take some notes. Put the notes into an outline and write the story. But Charlize, there is so much more here. There's so much more to her story that you can't fit it all into one book. It's impossible."

"Okay. Well, that's a good thing. So what has you upset?"

"So, she was married. Filed for divorce and left him. Bought a place, which is the very cabin I'm staying in."

"Okay. I'm following so far."

"There's a strange hospital stay document from New York here. And a condo in New York. And then there are copies of emails from some woman named Claudia. Claudia is warning Zetta to steer clear of Jed. And that Jed wants her, meaning Claudia."

"Okay. Still following."

"These emails are dated right around the time the cabin was finished."

"So Jed was having an affair?"

"That's the confusing part. I really don't know yet. I've been looking for the next dates in her journals, but I can't locate that specific one. I plan on thoroughly searching every inch of this cabin. She wrote about everything. It's impossible for her to not have written about an affair if he had one."

"Didn't you say that they were doing a long-distance relationship?"

"Yes. He stayed back in their hometown for his job. On the weekends, he would make sure to stay with Zetta."

"Hmmm. I bet you anything he had an affair, and this Claudia woman is the mistress. She's sending an email to Zetta out of jealousy and to prevent Jed from spending the weekend with her."

"And then here's the next strange part."

"I'm ready."

"I found court papers and legal docs for a restraining order."

"Against whom?"

"One of her stepdaughters."

"What?" Charlize questioned.

"Yes. But that's all there is. Just the legal doc. I'm not certain if it was filed or not, but it reveals some captivating details and helps me understand why she chose to end her marriage."

"Okay. Well..."

"There's just so much here. I thought I had a good idea of where to start, and now it's like I'm diving down some rabbit hole that's taking me where I never knew I needed to go. But I'm beginning to see some things and piece them together."

"Do you want me to help you with anything? Look something up? If you give me some names or something, I'll see what I can find. I know I'm not supposed to, but it sounds like you could use someone to take care of a few things while you get organized."

"I don't know what I need right now," I replied. "I appreciate that, though. And I'll definitely let you know as soon as I'm ready. But, yeah, this is a little bigger of a job than we anticipated."

"Okay, well, you keep doing what you're doing. Call me with anything at any time. Okay?"

"I will. Thank you, Charlize."

I ended the call and gazed at the table. Then a huge boom of thunder cracked, and lightning flashed, causing the lights to flicker.

I paused and stared around the cabin. The outside was already a dark green and, of course, I didn't have any candles or flashlights nearby. I grabbed my phone and connected it to the charger, hoping to charge it as much as I could.

Another flash of lightning and a rumble of thunder rattled the cabin.

After flickering one more time, the lights suddenly went out and plunged me into complete darkness.

I reached for my cell and put it in my pocket. I knew the layout of the cabin well, so I didn't need my phone's light. The rain fell, and the wind blew hard. Out the window I glimpsed Weston running around the yard, picking up empty pails and yard debris. He seemed like a nice man. I was pretty accurate in guessing his age. Up close, he looked more my age.

I walked down the hallway and opened the closet, using my phone for light. There were no flashlights or candles that I could see. I shut the door and entered Zetta's closet, facing a wall full of wicker baskets. I pulled them down one by one and looked at what was inside.

Most of it was backup items. Everything from makeup to hair care products and soaps. Inside one basket were pristine leather-bound journals, untouched and wrapped in plastic. I saved two, just in case I needed them to jot down my own notes. Maroon sharpie pens filled another basket. Extra maroon gloves. A basket of sunglasses. It was like she stocked up on all her favorite everyday items.

As the thunder rumbled again, I returned the basket to its place on the shelf and rushed to the kitchen to ensure the windows were secure. The gusts of wind were growing stronger and the rainfall was getting heavier. I made sure the porch doors were securely closed. Out the window, I caught sight of Weston walking towards the cabin.

I welcomed him inside by opening the porch door.

"You okay?" he asked. "We're in for a really intense storm. Wanted to make sure you were okay."

"I'm good. But the power is out."

"I don't have power either. Around here, it could be several days until it's restored."

"What? Really?"

He laughed.

"I'm serious. Welcome to the Northwoods, Isabel."

I stared at him in disbelief, desperately wishing he was joking. But he wasn't.

"Well, let me know if you need anything. Just bang on the porch door. The bell doesn't work. I'll keep an eye on your place, too. I think the most severe weather is going south of us. But we're still going to have some strong winds out of it."

"Okay, well, thank you."

"Okay. I'm going to brave the rain. Have a good night!"

I secured the door behind him and wandered into the kitchen.

I couldn't work on typing out Zetta's storyline

because of the power outage. I found a certain entry in one of her journals captivating, and couldn't wait to uncover the rest of the story. It felt like I was witnessing her life in slow motion. It was impossible for me not to anticipate her death as I read her journal entries, knowing the year she passed.

I jumped at another loud boom of thunder and made my way to the laundry room.

There have to be flashlights in here, I thought to myself.

I directed my phone light towards the shelving above the washer and dryer and read the labels on all the boxes. The orderliness of her home was impressive. It got me thinking about ways to organize my apartment in New York when I got back.

Flashlights!

"Yes!" I laughed as I pulled down the basket. I took a peek inside and removed one of the several flashlights. I observed another plastic container containing batteries, and a sense of relief washed over me. Well, this was going to help me through the first storm alone.

I returned to the kitchen and picked up the journal I was reading. I made the loveseat cozy and settled in to read with the flashlight.

Chapter 12

Zetta

I attempted to downplay my nervous excitement while returning to my hometown. This town had a nauseating effect on me. The true harm of things isn't apparent until they're no longer present. My moving away was a weight lifted from my shoulders. The weight of this place's negativity had slipped my mind over the last few months.

I prayed and took a deep breath, hoping I'd survive the weekend with Jed. At least we could stay inside and he'd take all the stress away again like he always does. I kept reminding myself that it was only one weekend. My divorce hearing would be the only reason I'd have to come back to this town again. Aside from that, it's good riddance. Jed's plan was to leave; all he needed was a job. With a baby on the way, this might be the motivation he needs to make that decision.

If I keep writing books, we'll have plenty of money to live on. If the next tour goes well, he might stay home and assist me in my work. We can raise our family together, with neither of us working outside the house.

As I entered the town, the level of excitement rose. I planned to make it here earlier, but I didn't factor in the road construction and detours. Since it was ten o'clock, I knew I would be surprising him before bedtime, not dinner.

I smiled as I looked at the bouquet of a dozen roses on the passenger seat. Life was going to feel whole. As soon as the light turned green, I turned left and proceeded down the side street towards his house.

There was a momentary feeling of nostalgia as I drove down the road, but it was overshadowed by memories of how life was when I lived here just a few months ago.

The butterflies in my stomach were almost too much to handle; then again, how should I feel when I see or think about the man who holds half my heart? The man I'm choosing to spend the rest of my life with.

I pressed the brake and turned into his driveway.

The lights were off and I smiled as I parked in front of his garage. I glanced around, but his truck was nowhere to be seen. I gathered the flowers, card, and wine and walked towards the door.

I pressed the doorbell and waited.

Nothing.

I pressed it a second time. I added a couple of knocks this time.

Nothing.

I looked at the house and saw no signs of activity.

As I walked back to the car, I thought about calling

him. It's possible that he got off work late and ended up at the grocery store. Another option is that he's watching a game at the bar.

I pulled out of his driveway and turned left, then took another left to circle back to town. While getting closer to the stop sign on the country road, I felt uncertain.

I could make another left and head to town, or I could go straight and drive past Claudia's house. When I thought about it, a lump formed in my throat. Claudia and I share a backstory. Unfortunately, it's not a good one. However, it wasn't entirely terrible either. I didn't necessarily dislike the woman. I just didn't like the fact that she gloated about Jed wanting her and her only.

She reached out to me via email a few times to keep me updated about their relationship. I read the emails, but didn't send a response. At the time of her emails Jed and I hadn't made anything official, so it wasn't my place to say anything. Besides, I was married but separated, and Jed was seeing who he wanted to see. Only after I filed for divorce did we begin to take our relationship more seriously. Ever since I submitted the papers, we've been spending more time together and talking on the phone non-stop.

It had been months since Claudia last emailed, leading me to completely forget about her until now. Jed never brought her up.

What if she was telling me the truth? What if Jed preferred being with her over me? But what if she was mistaken and had ulterior motives like the rest of the women in this town? That reason could very well be the true motivation behind her emails.

I glanced at the time.

Ten-thirty-seven.

I didn't turn on my blinker, just kept going straight.

I slowed my drive as I rounded the corner. The second house on the right belonged to her.

The sight of his red truck in her driveway caused my heart to race and a lump to form in my throat.

I crept by her house, noticing that all the lights were off, and found a spot to pull over down the road. I dried the few tears that fell and reflected on her emails. I went over them quickly, but not in great detail. Now I wondered what I'd missed.

I made a U-turn and paused before passing her house again. Glancing at my passenger seat, I noticed the flowers and the letter I had devoted so much time to writing. That one time when I expressed all my hopes and dreams for Jed and me as a couple.

I was in a state of confusion.

If he was already in a relationship with her, why was he discussing marriage with me?

I had a nauseating feeling in my stomach.

I'd spent hours driving just to see him. I'd dedicated countless days, weeks, and the past few months to being with him. We had spent the entire summer together. While he renovated my cabin, he slept in my bed each night. We made breakfasts and dinners together. Laughed as we enjoyed a bonfire in the early-morning hours. We've made detailed plans for our vacations, including our honeymoon.

We talked about our childhoods. Our fears, hopes,

and dreams.

At my lowest, he was there to lend a helping hand. He supported me and gathered my broken pieces to help me rebuild.

What did I overlook?

Out of all the women in town, why Claudia Tasley? I don't think he expected me to drive all the way over to his place. But that shouldn't matter if he wanted a future with me.

I knew I messed up in bringing her back into our lives, and now I was kicking myself and cursing my name. I'd received warnings about Claudia from other women. There were countless women who advised me about her. But I didn't listen.

"Don't tell her Jed is single. She will take him from you like she has everyone else's husband a time or two."

Most rumors are untrue. The truth is, the information about Claudia Tasley was valid. I suppose her emails were a warning to me to stay away. I'm certain that she knew Jed was spending an excessive amount of time with me, and she was not happy about it.

I was curious about the decrease in phone calls between Jed and me. Although it didn't appear significant, I sensed that something was off. I thought it was related to the long-distance relationship.

Maintaining a long-distance relationship becomes difficult when you're being intimate with another woman.

Tears streamed down my face as I let out a deep sigh. I took full responsibility for this mistake. If I hadn't called her and asked for help that day Jed and I might be together tonight, celebrating the beginning of our family.

Chapter 13

Isabel

I jumped up from the couch and ran to the stack of papers on the table to search for the restraining order form that Zetta had filled out. It was making sense! As I connected to another piece of her story, my excitement grew.

She loved Phil. She never wanted to leave him. Phil was entangled in a bitter custody war with his deranged ex-wife, who was hell-bent on tearing his life apart. Zetta just happened to marry him at the perfect time. When she put that ring on, she became the target for everything that was going to happen.

Phil had already seen two of his daughters brainwashed by his ex, and now he was going through the painful process of losing his stepdaughters. It's not surprising that he placed his daughters on pedestals and allowed them to do anything without consequences. He was caught in a dilemma with no favorable outcome. No matter what he chose, Zetta was going to be hurt.

His ex-wife used the girls as pawns to destroy

Phil's life. Because of his stable household, the courts denied her custody of all the girls. Destroying their marriage was all she needed to do to claim the castle. And that's exactly what she did from the inside out.

Phil and Zetta's blissful marriage and flawless family life ended when they became pawns in his ex's sadistic and twisted game. The children were employed as weapons. It's expected that the girls will follow their mother's demands. Their goal was to earn Zetta's affection and approval. Their mother's venom terrified them, but they played their roles flawlessly.

While going through the pile of papers, I came across Claudia's emails and paused. I despised that woman even though I had no connection to her. Her words felt as painful as a box cutter slashing my skin. She knew Jed was with Zetta. She knew! It was right there in black and white, from her email address. Jealousy was evident in every one of her emails. And the threats to ruin Zetta's life if she didn't leave Jed alone. Who did this woman think she was?

The journal entries revealed that Zetta's life was rapidly spiraling out of control. Her divorce. The pregnancy. The fact that Jed's truck was at Claudia's house. And the restraining order.

I settled into the chair and positioned the flashlight to read the notes.

"...Reason for divorce: To get away from Phil's daughters and their vengeance towards me. The lies perpetuated by his daughters have had far-reaching consequences on my life, relationships, career, and marriage. Phil has done nothing wrong, but his daughters have intentionally undermined me. I simply long to have my life returned to me. All I desire is to regain my happiness."

In the succeeding paragraph, she sought a restraining order against his twelve-year-old daughter. Surveillance cameras were placed in the house and recorded the daughter tampering with Zetta's morning protein shake by adding floor cleaner. Another video showed the same daughter putting broken glass in Zetta's shoes. Numerous videos captured the daughter damaging Zetta's belongings in the home.

Zetta had a good reason to want to leave. Who would stay?

I leaned back in the chair and sighed. Her only desire was to live peacefully, yet accusations were constantly hurled at her. I found it incomprehensible that a child who posed such a threat was never held accountable. Zetta's cry for help fell on deaf ears. Then Claudia came in and snatched away the only happiness she had felt in ages.

At least she had her baby. There was a single positive element in her life.

Chapter 14

Zetta

As I sat across from Phil, I casually sipped from my glass of ice water. It felt strange to be back in this house. But I didn't want him to know where my cabin was, so this was the alternative.

"She promises she will stop lying and work on her behavior," he continued. "I didn't realize things were that bad. I apologize for not listening to you, and if I could go back in time I would. Just so I could make it all right."

"Phil, I told you repeatedly. I tried to show you the videos. The messages people left me on voicemail. I know you were stuck in the middle, but in all honesty, doing nothing for so many years, I don't see her changing."

He nodded.

"I just want you back home. It's not the same without you here. So much of this is my fault, and I just want you back home, Zetta. Please come back home. I miss you."

I fought my emotions and fixed my gaze on the portraits lining the wall. I missed him so much, but I couldn't go back to that life. I would never force him to choose between me and his children.

"Zetta, I'm begging you. I'll go to counseling. I'll do whatever I need to just so you'll come back home."

"Phil, this is not a safe environment."

"I thought about that, too. The girls want to move in with their mother. Fine. They can move. I'm done fighting. In their eyes, I will forever be the bad guy. Their mother has too much control over them."

"I don't want you to let the girls move on account of me. That's not fair."

"What's not fair is what their mother is doing. And I can't stop that. No matter what I do, I can't prevent her from brainwashing them. It's clear to me now. All the damage she caused all these years. I see it. I know we can't go back in time, but I can't see myself living without you."

He inched closer and placed his hand on my knee.

"Zetta, please," he begged. "Give me one more try. One. That's all I'm asking. Just one more try. I am capable of being the husband you need."

"It's not just that. There's this entire town. The lies your daughters have told. People think I abused your kids. Some people believe that you want me to leave."

"People think a lot of things. I'm aware of what has been said. Hell, I know what your aunt said. I heard her. It's astonishing that she chose to side with a child instead of us, considering you're her niece. Instead of approaching us directly, she chose to believe a child's lies."

I dried the tears that had started to fall.

"I know, Zetta. I will always be on your side. The opinions and feelings of others are of no importance to me. You leaving opened a lot of eyes, especially my own. And things are going to change. If the kids don't like it then they don't need to visit. I mean that sincerely."

There are instances when people should be given a second opportunity. I've known all along that Phil was not responsible for what was happening. It's not our fault for ending up in the situation we were thrown into. Our main focus was simply on surviving.

I brought my bags back home in small increments over the following months, but left the bulk of my belongings at the cabin. It provided a sense of security in case things took a turn for the worse. In one of our discussions, I mentioned to him that the girls could still come to visit him as planned, and I'd use those weekends to concentrate on my writing at my cabin. Then we'd have the alternate weekends to ourselves.

I just had to figure out how to tell him about the baby.

Chapter 15

Isabel

I arrived in Zetta's hometown and drove through the residential areas. There wasn't much to the small town. The area consisted of various factories, a school, two gas stations, and an endless number of bars.

The power wasn't expected to be turned on for another 48 hours at the cabin. I decided it was the right time to visit Claudia in person. I gathered the emails and notes with addresses. I was familiar with Claudia on a level that she likely didn't anticipate. Confronting people wasn't something I felt comfortable doing. But this called for a leap outside of my comfort zone.

I took a left at the stoplight, turned left on the next road, and went straight at the stop sign. I slowed down just as Zetta had the night she drove by looking for Jed. Zetta's journals accurately described the appearance of Claudia's house. A yellow house with brown shutters, oversized porch with a swing and a brick patio out the back. I was relieved to see that she hadn't moved in all these years, as the sign "Welcome to the Tasleys'" was still visible at the end of the driveway.

There was a moment of hesitation before I drove into her driveway. As I moved closer to the garage, my heart started racing. My stomach churned with nausea, mirroring the exact symptoms Zetta felt upon seeing Jed's truck in this driveway all those years ago.

I parked my car, took my notepad and pen, and headed up the sidewalk. Standing on her porch, I felt sparks of anger ignite inside me. As I knocked on the door, I reminded myself that I was doing this for Zetta.

I waited for a few minutes before a woman with blond hair opened the door and smiled at me. It was apparent that she attempted to conceal her gray as she got older. I noticed her green eyes were lackluster, and she turned out to be shorter than I had pictured.

"Hello?"

"Are you Claudia Tasley?" I asked.

She nodded and smiled. "I am."

I stared into the eyes of the Claudia Tasley, the very woman who had stolen Jed Conley from Zetta all those years ago.

"Do I know you?" she questioned.

I shook my head.

"I'm Isabel Vinson. I'm an investigative journalist from New York working on uncovering the story of Zetta Castellan."

I witnessed her face losing color as she gripped the doorframe. I opened my notepad and continued talking.

"May I ask you a few questions? Would that be okay?"

"Um. Sure. I guess." I could feel her discomfort, which brought me some relief.

"I just have a few." I smiled at her. "I'm sure you know she passed a few months ago."

Claudia nodded.

"I've been assigned to her story and just want to make sure the details are accurate. She received emails from you that mentioned someone named Jed Conley. Does his name ring a bell?"

She stared at me for a few seconds before nodding.

"Okay. Is it accurate to say that you and he were together for almost a decade?"

"Um. I guess I don't know exactly. Very well could be."

I made a note of it on my notepad.

"In 2013 you were aware that Zetta and Jed were in a relationship, correct? If you don't recall, I can grab my case file."

"I think we're done here," she intoned, trying to smile.

"Are you sure? I really don't want the story to include any inaccuracies. Was it true that you were incredibly jealous of their relationship?"

She slammed the door in my face. I guess I had gotten to her! I grinned while walking back to my car. All I'd wanted to do was remind Claudia of the past, nothing more.

Chapter 16

Zetta

I found myself seated across from Iris Do-herbleek, the woman who had authority over my career as an author. Smiling, she scribbled notes and discussed the events scheduled for next year. I did my best to pay attention, but everything was a blur. It takes true resilience to remain strong when everything is falling apart.

"Zetta? Are you okay?"

I paused, blinked a few times, and then took a deep breath.

"You don't look so well. You feeling okay?"

With great difficulty, I whispered, "Iris—" amidst the tears.

"Oh dear," she said as she stood and walked to the other side of the table. "Honey, what is it? Please tell me. Whatever it is, it's okay. Not all of these events are necessary. We can downsize a few."

I couldn't hold back my tears as she hugged me, shaking my head in disbelief. After receiving a Kleenex from her and allowing myself to cry, I sat upright and dried my eyes.

"I'm pregnant," I blurted.

"Oh? Congratulations!" She beamed.

I shook my head. "It's a mess." My entire story spilled out as I described how everything was in complete disarray.

As she leaned back in her chair, she stared at me and nodded her head. Rather than canceling my contract, she surprised me by placing her hand on my knee and speaking softly.

"Zetta, I'm here for you. Whatever you need, I'm ready to help you."

It had been so long since I'd felt this way, but having someone to talk to brought me a sense of relief. I felt like Iris heard me and listened to what I was saying. As our afternoon-long conversation came to a close, her final words echoed in my mind.

"I know the perfect family."

From that day forward, Iris and I had a secret. A secret we would take to our graves.

Chapter 17

Isabel

I paused at the end of Claudia's driveway and headed back the way I came. I had passed Jed's house on the way here and I wanted it to be my next stop. After passing the stop sign, I turned right at the next one and pulled into his driveway.

I was excited and nervous about talking to him. Zetta wasn't here to fill in the gaps, and I knew he could tell his side and help in that way. I stepped from my car and walked up to the door and knocked.

"Can I help you?" A man answered the door.

"Jed? Jed Conley?" I asked.

"Um, no." The guy gave me a puzzled look. "Jed is no longer here."

"Oh, I'm sorry," I replied. "Do you know where I could reach him? Or where he moved to?"

A small smile appeared on the man's face. "East-field cemetery. You'll find him under the red oak tree in the far back."

"Excuse me?"

"Lady, he died a few years ago. Unless you have some form of spiritual power, you're probably not going to be able to reach him."

"Thank you," I replied. "I had no idea he'd passed."

"Good day," the man said as he closed the door.

Once I got back to my car, I left the driveway and immediately called Charlize.

"You're not going to believe this," I said when she answered.

"What?"

"Jed Conley died a few years ago."

"Really?" she questioned. "You know, something told me to check the records before you drove all the way over there. I should've listened to my gut."

"That's okay. I also visited Claudia and she very forcefully closed the door in my face, not wanting to answer any more of my questions."

"Well, can you blame her?" Charlize laughed.

"Not really. I guess that makes sense now that both Zetta and Jed have passed. It probably made her relive the past in a much stronger way. Oh, hey, can I call you back? My mom is calling on the other line."

"Yeah, absolutely. Talk to you soon."

"Hey, Mom." I smiled as I greeted her.

"Hey, honey. How are you? Haven't talked to you in a few days."

"I'm doing well. Just working on the assignment."

"And how is it going?"

"Well, it's going."

"Who are you writing about this time? I don't know if I ever asked you before you left."

"It was last-minute, so I didn't have a clear un-derstanding of who it was until I arrived. I'm in Wisconsin."

"Oh okay," she replied.

"Yeah. This woman had a cabin here. Well, her home is here and I'm staying in her home while I read her journals and take notes. I think I'll be here another month or two at the most."

"Okay. Is it a nice place?"

"Oh, Mom. You would absolutely love it here. It's the perfect vacation getaway. In the middle of the woods. Small town and oh so quiet. I'll share some pics with you. The cabin is gorgeous."

"Who's the person?"

"Zetta Castellan. She's an author who—"

"Zetta?" she repeated.

"Yes. Zetta Castellan. Her books are—"

"I know who she is," my mom interrupted. "Um, I had no idea you were—"There was a long, awkward silence.

"Mom?"

"Sorry, honey. I think I stayed up a little too late last night. I need to rest for a bit. Can I call you later?"

"Yes. Yes. We'll talk later."

I set my phone on the center console just as it rang again.

"Hey, Charlize. I was just going to call you back."

"Isabel. I just had a strange call from an attorney in Wisconsin. You're supposed to give him a call back. What's that about? He said it's a personal matter."

"I have no idea. Text me his number. I'll call him or try again when I get back to the cabin."

"You sure everything is okay? He made it sound like this was urgent."

"Charlize, I don't know anyone from Wisconsin. So

I'm just as confused as you are. And why would they call you?"

"This is your place of employment. That's how he got the number here. He even knew you were in Wisconsin and stopped by the place you're staying. Strange. Well, call me back and let me know everything is okay at least. You don't have to tell me details if it's a personal matter. Just want to make sure you're okay."

"Yes, of course," I replied, then we hung up.

Did Claudia do something? Call her attorney on me for asking questions? That's the first thing that popped into my head. Claudia Tasley. She wasted no time trying to cover her tracks.

Chapter 18

Zetta

Deceiving Phil about my two-month stay in New York was another self-inflicted blow to my soul. I was lucky enough to not have any visible signs of pregnancy. I could wear my wardrobe with no difficulties. However, Iris had worries about the upcoming two months. I would one day wake up with a rounded belly, and then I'd have no choice but to tell Phil. It made sense to head to New York for the delivery now, in order to maintain privacy.

Phil and I had been doing very well. When his daughters came to visit I would dedicate those weekends to writing in my cabin. The schedule was working out wonderfully. Jed stopped trying to reach out to me after two weeks of no response. I was too upset to have a conversation with him, and wasn't interested in hearing any more excuses or empty promises.

However, my curiosity got the better of me. I'd drive past his house and then past Claudia's. His truck was parked at her house more frequently than at his own. After a few months, I quit looking for him. I'd had the answer all along. He chose her, and it devastated me. But I had to keep it to myself. The combination of a broken heart, random crying, and pregnancy made me feel drained.

"How was your flight?" Iris asked as she escorted me to the elevator.

"Nice. Very nice. I've never flown first class before."

"Well, only the best for you and the wee one."

I tried to smile, but struggled with every part of my reason for being in New York. Was I doing the right thing? I knew I'd be able to give my baby a good home. There was no question about that. What I did question was how Phil would react. And how the girls could ruin the life of an innocent person. I regret to admit that, even though my career was flourishing, I didn't feel prepared for motherhood. I don't know what was causing the feelings. Had Jed stayed, maybe things would be different. But I couldn't bring a child into a broken home.

As soon as I met the parents, I knew they were the perfect match. Both were college professors, and they couldn't have children of their own. They'd been trying for years, and now that they were in their early forties they had given up on ever having a child. Perhaps there was a purpose to this relationship with Jed. This baby would have the comfort of a stable and loving home, free from any disruptions or uncertainties.

"What did Phil say when you left?" Iris asked.

"Well, he knows I'm working on a book deadline, so it's the same ol' "Good luck". He didn't ask questions," I replied.

"Well, your due date is in three weeks. So by the time you get situated, the baby should be arriving. Then you can take the rest of the time to heal and relax before you head back."

"I just want to thank you again, Iris. I've never really had anyone to talk to, and I can't even express how appreciative I am of you. You've been incredibly supportive and never made me feel like a failure."

"Oh, honey, you are not a failure. Each day, numerous women are faced with the same circumstances as you. It brings me joy to know that we can support another couple and ensure the baby grows up in a fantastic home. Rest assured, I won't bring this up with anyone else. It's just you and me."

You and me.

I'm familiar with that line, having heard it from many people. Phil. Jed. The only difference with Iris is that I believed her. I could always count on her.

After Iris departed, I settled into the condo and took in the city view. The view was nice, and the building was more upscale than I'd expected. I felt safe knowing that the building was secure and visitor access was only granted with my permission.

"Hey, darling," Phil answered when I called. "You get all settled in?"

"Yeah. This place is nice, Phil. Wow."

"Did they arrange for you to stay in a penthouse, with a view of the Towers?"

"Not exactly. But close," I replied.

"Well, I already miss you. These two months had better go by fast," he said. "Maybe we can sneak a dinner in somewhere or something. To give you a little break."

"Phil," I said. "You know I'm on a deadline. There will be no dinner break or shopping of any sort until the book is complete. Publisher's orders."

"You excel at working under pressure, especially with tight deadlines."

"Ugh, I know. I hate them and love them all at the same time."

Chapter 19

Isabel

I turned over in bed to answer my phone when it rang. It was Charlize. After the visit to Zetta's hometown, the drive back to the cabin felt like it took forever. I took a moment to visit Eastfield Cemetery. Jed's grave was right where that man said it would be. The year of death engraved on the tombstone was 2021. I captured a few photos on my cellphone that I planned to print and leave at Zetta's cabin, alongside her other mementos.

"Hey, Charlize," I greeted.

"Isabel. You need to call that attorney. He called again this morning," she said right off the bat. "I don't mean to sound harsh, but he was a little testy with me since you hadn't called him yet."

"I got back late and thought I'd call him today. It's only eight-thirty."

"Yeah, well, it must be something important if he's calling so early."

"Okay, I'll call him right now. And then I'll let you know what it's about 'cause I'm curious too. I have no idea why an attorney would be calling me. The one thing I thought about on my drive back here was Claudia. My bet is that she called someone after my unexpected visit, since I probably brought up a past she thought was long dead."

"Oh, maybe," she said. "You might be right. Serves her right, though, if she turned her back on Zetta like that and took Jed from her, even though she had a husband."

"And kids. Don't forget her kids."

"Kids!" she practically screeched. "Oh, hell no."

"Yeah. Okay, I'll call him and let you know what's going on."

"Thanks, Isabel."

I stepped out of bed and slipped on my shoes. I didn't arrive back here until late last night and was too tired to bring everything in from the car.

"Hey, Isabel!" Weston waved from the porch of his house as I crossed the driveway to my car.

"Hi, Weston!" I shouted back, hoping he'd stay there and not venture over here for small talk. I looked like a mess and could practically feel the taste of my morning breath. I quickly gathered my belongings and made my way back into the cabin.

I left everything on the table and went to shower. I had a list of things to research, look up, organize, and write. I laughed to myself, realizing that the life of a writer was a never-ending journey. I thoroughly enjoyed doing all the things.

I stepped from the shower, dried my hair, and slipped into another outfit of Zetta's. Black leggings, black turtleneck, beige leather vest, and some black ankle boots. I pulled my hair back into a low ponytail before sitting at her makeup station. I put on moisturizer, maroon mascara, and lip gloss.

Upon opening the drawer, I examined her assortment of jewelry and settled on a square titanium watch with a white band, along with some small gold hoop earrings. A combination of simplicity and elegance.

I started feeling more at ease in her house and became quite proficient at finding things, like her journals. There were three shelves left for me to read, but I would get to them when the time was right. I prepared a cup of chai and stepped onto the porch. While sitting down, I picked up a book from her coffee table and read the back cover.

Mornings on the Porch, by Nancy Kuykendall. Sometimes an ordinary day, or moment or event, can suddenly take an extraordinary turn and come to mean more, or teach you more, than you ever would have expected. Have you ever had a mundane day turn into something spectacular? Have you ever been full of an anger you couldn't let go of, then in a moment were freed from it? Do you have precious memories held deep inside? Have you ever had to give up a dream? Have you ever achieved a goal or dream? Have you ever suffered pain or a hurt so intense you didn't believe you could get through another day, yet you did? Have you loved and lost? Have you ever had strong opinions, yet find yourself in the minority? Have you ever felt you don't belong? Have you ever experienced small miracles? Have you ever been touched by God and received joy no matter your circumstances? *Mornings on the Porch* is all of these stories and more. Life as it touches us.

A life-long musician, after retiring from a thirty-hear teaching career Nancy pursued her desire to write. Her inspiration comes from her experiences, surroundings, circumstances, life events, people and pets, and her relationship with God.

I opened the cover and noticed the book was a signed edition. As I sipped my tea, I relaxed and turned the page.

"Knock-knock."

I reacted by swiftly spinning around to face the door. After setting the book on the table, I went to open the porch door.

"Sorry. Didn't mean to startle you," Weston said as I stepped outside.

I smiled. "I was just getting lost in a book. What's up?"

"Say, yesterday there was a man that showed up here. Said he needed to talk to you, that it was urgent. He left his card for me to give to you," he said as he handed me a business card. "I knew you were staying alone, so I thought it was strange to see him over here."

"Well, thank you. I've been expecting him, actually. Thank you for letting me know he stopped by."

"You okay? You got home late last night."

"I'm great, yes. Just visited some folks for the project I'm working on."

"Okay. Well, have a good day," he said as he turned to walk away. He turned around to glance at me again as he kept walking.

I stared at the business card and grabbed my cell phone.

"Say," Weston said as he stopped abruptly and turned around again. "You want to have dinner tonight? It's okay if you want to say no. Just thought I'd ask to see if you might want to join me."

"I would really like that." I smiled at him. "What should I bring?"

"Just yourself," he replied, grinning. "Seven o'clock too late?"

"Seven is perfect."

"Okay. See you then. Have a good day, Isabel."

"Isabel," a man's voice answered when I dialed the number on the business card. "I've been trying to get a hold of you."

"I hear that. Sorry, I had a few errands to run, and I'm just getting unpacked again. What can I help you with?"

"Well, I was hoping to meet with you in person. We can meet in town or I can stop by Zetta's house."

"Um, you can stop here if that works. I'll be here all day."

"Sounds good. How about in one hour? Does that work?"

"Um, yes. That should be perfect. Can I ask what this is about?"

"Oh, it's nothing I can discuss over the phone," he explained. "Nothing bad, if that's what you're inquiring. Good news. All good news. I'll see you in one hour."

Chapter 20

Zetta

11 Years Later

I put my car in drive and stepped on the gas. I needed to get out of this town, away from this house. Away from everyone. Things were going well for a while, but gradually returned to how they used to be. The backstabbing, deception, and speculation. I had reached a point where I was fed up with the rumors. Not a single person knew the truth. Every adult avoided coming directly to Phil or me. They fell for all the lies his daughters were telling.

I'd had enough.

I was glad that I'd kept my cabin. I had considered selling the property for a few years, but a gut feeling urged me to hold on to it. Since I rarely set foot in the big house, I could sell it. My cabin is where I spend most of my time.

I think about Jed often. More than I should. The slip of paper with his phone number he gave me years ago is still in my wallet. There's been many times that I want to call him up, but I stop myself. I can't go through another goodbye. I have the hope that he will understand it one day.

There are so many nights that I cry and wish it was his arms I was wrapped in. He knew how to make everything okay. Despite his empty promises, I believed he had good intentions. If only things had turned out differently. I regret not contacting him about Claudia instead of ignoring his messages. Maybe it wasn't at all what I was thinking, but seeing his truck in her driveway hurt.

I think back to what life could have been like had Jed and I worked out. Would we be living our happily-ever-after like we'd talked about? Celebrating milestones, anniversaries, birthdays, and family vacations. I look back and see all the years we've missed out on together. I haven't seen him in eleven years. Eleven years of time we lost out on.

Despite my efforts, I find it hard to stop feeling resentful about what happened.

I should've run after him. I should've fought for him, but he never fought for me. Both of us gave up too soon.

I arrived at my cabin four hours later, went straight to bed, and sobbed over my chaotic life. I just want to be happy. It was becoming too much to ask. I thought my weekends spent away from home were acceptable. But this week, Phil decided that it's not working out. That I should be there with the family if I want us to be a family.

And that's the issue. I *want* to be a family. It's his girls who are against the idea of us being a family. I'm just tired of it all. It's an unbreakable cycle that will persist until one of us calls it off. Despite the urge to cry, it's easier to leave this time compared to the last time.

Last year Iris retired, and I've been fortunate to have an amazing new assistant, Catherine, to work with. Since I've cut back on my public appearances, she's got it pretty easy now. I have a list of book ideas I'd love to sit and write before my time is up. So that is my new goal, along with trying to figure out this new life. I'm ready to keep a more private life.

Chapter 21

Isabel

As Iris arrived in the driveway, I hurriedly applied lotion to my hands. I was surprised to see her and stepped outside to greet her.

"Iris," I smiled. "I wasn't expecting you. What a nice surprise."

"Well, it's nice to see you again. You look—" She paused and stared at me. "You look gorgeous, Isabel. Remarkably gorgeous," she murmured as she followed me into the cabin. "I see you've made yourself at home. Good. Very good."

"Oh, yes. Excuse the tables and stacks of everything, but it is organized!" I laughed. "I've been making progress and have a good start to her story."

Iris smiled as she stepped inside and admired the organized stacks. She lightly touched a few of the journals.

"I numbered them for easier reference," I explained when I saw her looking at the post-it notes.

"I see. And there he is now," Iris mentioned as she looked over my shoulder.

I looked back and saw a black SUV coming up the

driveway.

"Mr. Livingston has arrived."

"He's the attorney, I assume?"

"Yes. Did he not introduce himself on the phone to you? Don't take it personally. He needs to retire like the rest of us. Great man. Very, very good attorney. Mr. Livingston!" Iris exclaimed as she opened the door and stepped outside.

"And you must be Isabel," he said as he extended his hand. "I'm Mark Livingston. And this is my assistant, Meredith."

"C'mon in," Iris invited as she held open the door. "Is the porch okay?"

"Oh, yes," Mark replied.

As Mark and Meredith entered the cabin, I shook their hands before they settled on the porch's wicker loveseat. Mark placed his briefcase on the table and rested his hands in his lap, Iris and I facing him in separate wicker chairs.

"I want to thank you again for meeting with me, Isabel. We won't be long. Just have a few papers to go over and we'll be on our way." He smiled.

I nodded while giving Iris a look of confusion. A smile crossed her face as she nodded briefly and then turned to Mark.

"In the matter of the estate of Zetta Castellan," he began as he picked up a document and raised his glasses to read. "This property that we're uh... This cabin sits on twenty-eight acres. So this cabin and the pole shed. Everything from this side of the iron fence is the property of Zetta Castellan. All items currently in the shed have been accounted for. I have the list here," he said as he handed a sheet to

Iris and one to me. "The items in the shed include her car. Um, a Lexus. The year looks to be 2018. That is paid in full. This cabin and all items inside, including books, clothing, furniture. The list goes on. Here is a copy for each of you as well."

I stole a quick look at Iris while she was engrossed in the document. While Mark spoke, I scanned each sheet in silence.

"There is uh—" He paused. "Two. Looks like two checking accounts here. One savings account and some other miscellaneous accounts as well. They appear to all be at the same financial institution. Here's a copy of that for both of you."

He fumbled through his briefcase and pulled out a folder.

"Zetta had a few life insurance policies on herself. Here is that documentation," he said as he handed us each a folder. "You can just call the number on the business card for that. You will need original copies of her death certificate, though. I think we have that with us. Meredith, you have that, right?"

Meredith nodded, retrieved a manila folder, and passed it to me.

"You should have all the certificates you need. She made sure there would be plenty of originals for proof of her death."

"Mr. Livingston, I'm just a little confused as to why I'm being handed all these things. I'm just here to—"

"My apologies." He glanced at Iris and gave her a look of confusion.

"She isn't aware of that, Mark."

"I see. Okay. Isabel, I understand why you're feeling confused. What you are holding in your hands are the forms for—"

"Oh, wait." Iris raised her hand. "I just have one quick call to make before we get to that part. Excuse me for just one moment."

I watched Iris step outside and make a phone call.

"This is a lovely cabin," Meredith said. "Decorated so nicely. I can't help but feel like I'm on a movie set or something."

I smiled. "Yeah, I feel the same way. It's just as she left it. I haven't moved a thing. And I've made sure to put everything back in its place, just as she had it."

Iris smiled and reentered the room, taking a seat. She held the phone up so we all could see. "Okay."

"Mom?" I said when I glanced at Iris' phone and saw who she had called.

"Hey, honey. Oh, it's nice to see you."

"What's going on?" I asked as I looked at all of them.

Iris nodded at Mark to proceed.

"Okay. Thank you for joining us, Mrs. Vinson. As I was saying, those forms I gave to you have all the information you'll need to switch Zetta's accounts over. You have her original death certificates. Every account will need an original."

"This still doesn't make sense. This was not part of the job description."

Mark smiled and continued. "As the only heir to her estate, Isabel Vinson, you are now the owner of all of Zetta's assets, including this cabin. Everything. All of it."

"What? How can I be an heir? I didn't even know the woman. I'm just here to write her story."

"Isabel, honey. Please let them explain," my mom

said.

"Isabel, you are aware you're adopted, right?" Meredith asked.

I nodded. "Yes. My parents always let me know."

"Well, Zetta is your birth mother," Meredith continued. "She's been following you all these years, and when you began your journalism career she was overjoyed. You inherited her passion for writing. After she became ill, she documented her last wishes in case she didn't have the chance to meet you."

I leaned back in my chair, unsure if I was hearing her correctly.

"Are you okay, hon?" Iris asked as she placed a hand on my knee.

"Honey, I wanted to be there for this but—"

"It's okay, Mom. I'm just in shock right now."

Meredith smiled as she glanced around at all of us. "There's not a lot more to what she told us. You are the only biological child she has. Her wish was for you to receive everything. Is there anything you would like to ask at this point?"

I laughed. "I have an overwhelming number of things to process, and no idea where to begin. It feels surreal."

"I know it does. And it will for quite some time. Mark and I are both here if you have any questions. Our cards are in the folder you have."

"That's all we have," Mark added. "If there's nothing more, we will see ourselves out. Isabel." Mark smiled. "You look just like her. Identical to her, right down to your mannerisms."

"Mom, you knew about Zetta?" I asked after Mark and Meredith left the cabin.

"Honey, I did. However, she asked me to keep her secret until she felt ready to meet you. I would have loved to tell you sooner, but I had to respect her wishes."

I nodded.

"You knew?" I looked at Iris.

She nodded.

"And you had to keep it secret."

She nodded again.

"Well, I can't be upset with anyone. It is what it is. I think I just need time to adjust to all that info. That was a lot."

"Call me later, honey, okay?" my mom said.

"I will." I smiled. "I love you, Mom."

"Love you, too."

I watched Iris leave and wandered into the living room to sit on the couch. I leaned back and closed my eyes.

Chapter 22

Zetta

This year, our daughter turned thirteen. I can't believe 2012 is here already. I officially have a teenager. Well, sort of. I get to see her growing up through pictures. Her adoptive mother has been going the extra mile by keeping me updated on milestones and fun moments through letters. Just for this reason alone, I can't wait to get my mail. Iris was right. The family she had was exactly what I wanted for my baby.

Each year I buy a small cake, light some candles, and hope she knows how much I love her. I know she's doing well. Her parents send updates and photos. There's a dedicated locked chest in my closet that I've set aside for her. I've included personal journals written for her. Some day she will read them, and I want her to know I think about her all day long, every single day. She's turning into a wonderful young lady, and I can't wait to meet her when she's older and the time is right.

Phil and I have agreed to try yet again. I feel compelled to give him numerous chances, even though

I don't understand why. I always seem to get hurt in the end. Without fail, the ending is always the same. I should know better by now.

I saw Jed the other day in the grocery store parking lot. It took everything in me to stay in my car and not race after him. His appearance has improved with age, and he looks even more handsome now. I had a flood of nostalgic thoughts and considered reaching out to him while I was in town, but decided against it. If I wanted to work on things with Phil, I had to leave the past in the past. And that included Jed Conley.

Chapter 23

Isabel

I jumped from the couch and raced to the kitchen to check the time on the microwave. Six-seventeen. My heart was racing as I fought with the grogginess of waking from a dead sleep. I half thought I missed the dinner with Weston.

The day felt like a blur. I wanted to forget life for a few hours and was now more excited than ever to get out of the cabin. I wasn't sure what he had planned for dinner, so I grabbed a bowl from the cupboard, opened the fridge, and make a quick raw veggie bowl. I grabbed a bottle of hot sauce and ranch dressing as well.

I know he told me not to bring anything, but I would like to bring something. Besides, if I didn't like what he was cooking at least I had my veggies.

I cleaned up around the cabin for a bit, then freshened up before making my way across the driveway. Weston was arranging items on a table near the fire pit.

"Hey, neighbor!" I smiled. "I know you said not to bring anything, but I had to bring something."

He laughed. "I figured as much. I hope you love brats or steak. I made them both. And—" He smiled as he lifted a glass baking dish. "Roasted baby red potatoes."

"Wow, you went all out," I replied.

"Not really. When you can't decide what you want to eat, you just make everything. Then you have leftovers and don't have to cook for a few days. Kind of a win-win."

"Okay, yes. Very true," I said as I placed the bowl on the table.

We sat around the fire, ate dinner, and chatted until we felt raindrops.

"I didn't think it was supposed to rain," I said as I glanced up at the sky.

"That's the thing about living in the Northwoods. We get these pop-up showers that never show on the radar."

"Really?"

He nodded. "Oh, yes. It could be sunny over there across the lake while you're experiencing a torrential rain. Happens all the time."

"Good to know." I grinned. "I can help you bring all this inside."

We stood and went to the table, collecting dishes and trays. I followed Weston to the side of the house and walked inside as he held the door open.

"Kitchen is just off to the right," he said as he followed me. "We can just set it all on the counter. I can put it all away later."

"You sure?"

"Absolutely. I'll go grab the last few items. Be right back. Make yourself at home."

I washed and dried my hands, then wandered through the kitchen into the living room. In the middle of the wall on the right side there was a rock fireplace that went up to the ceiling. On either side of the fireplace there were bookshelves built into the walls. The shelves were filled with books, with a few photos placed sporadically.

Positioned in front of the fireplace there was an L-shaped sofa, a charming coffee table, and the most stunning rug I had ever laid eyes on. The shade was a blend of black, ivory, and rusty orange. As I looked around, I saw more rustic orange elements scattered around the room. The room had a cozy, warm, and inviting feel to it.

I moved to the opposite side of the room, where two recliners were placed with a table in the middle. On the table there was a lamp shaped like a bear, and a pile of books topped with a candle.

"I haven't touched this room since he passed."

I shifted my gaze towards Weston.

"It's just as he left it. Every item. I try to put things back where he had them."

"I've been doing the same at Zetta's. Keeping things how she left them."

"I'm just not ready to change it up. You know?" He tucked his hands into his front pockets and glanced around the room. "It's like he's still here. I can still see him sitting in that chair right there, reading. He loved to read, as you can tell by the bookcase. This isn't even all his books. There's more upstairs in his library."

"Library?"

"Well, it's another bedroom that was converted

into a library. The entire room is lined with shelves and then he added some center bookshelves. So, it really feels like a small library."

"I love the way he decorated. It's very cozy."

"I don't think he decorated." Weston laughed. "He had someone else with more experience do that for him. I saw his last place, and that was nowhere near as cozy and inviting as this place."

"I see."

"Yeah."

I took a step closer to the shelf and my eyes were immediately drawn to one of the portraits. I quickly scanned the other side of the fireplace and a couple of the photos took my breath away for a moment.

"Why does he have framed photos of Zetta? This is her, right?"

Weston inched closer to the shelves. "Is that who that is? I wasn't sure who it was, or who anyone else is on these shelves."

"Yeah. That's her."

"Well, he does have her books. A lot of them, actually. This section here is all Zetta Castellan. You know, I didn't realize it was her who lived next door. I didn't learn that until she passed. I never got to meet her, and I was here a lot."

Maybe it was normal for people to have portraits of their favorite authors on their shelves. Zetta also had possessed many framed photos of authors. It must've been something that generation loved to have. It's definitely not something that crossed my mind to include on my shelves.

"You know," Weston said as he stared at her photo, then back to me. "You look a lot like her in this picture. Look at this one," he said as he reached for her photo.

My throat tightened, and I held my breath.

"I have to go. Thank you for dinner, Weston. I appreciate it."

"What?" He placed the photo back on the shelf and followed me to the door. "Did I say something wrong?"

"No." I shook my head. "I just need to go. Thank you again."

Chapter 24

Zetta

When dinner was done, I stood in the kitchen and stared at the mess. The center island was covered with dinner plates, food, and glasses. I watched as Phil and the girls gathered in the living room to watch something on television. I found myself in the role of a maid. The hired caregiver. The doormat.

Since 2013, Jed and I grew closer after he came to my book signing in New York. He had attended all the other signings in New York. Having him back in my life after all these years was a nice feeling. Since Phil stopped attending my signings, Jed moved some of his stuff into my New York condo. We spent a lot of time ordering takeout, catching up on lost years, and making plans for the future. His words felt different this time, unlike before. Two years had passed, and reality was setting in.

It was Jed who got the first look at my manuscript drafts. Whenever I had a crazy story idea, he was the one I would bounce it off of. He helped with the plot holes and storylines, and even had some great ideas of his own. We had been back and forth to my cabin, staying in the house, and even having fun redecorating the place.

I transferred the remaining food into containers and placed them in the refrigerator. Loading the dishwasher brought tears to my eyes. I loved my life. I loved Phil. As the girls grew older, their troublesome behavior, which had caused torment for years, was diminishing. Especially this year. But I knew it was too late. I was in love with Jed. To be honest, I don't think I ever fell *out* of love with Jed.

"You know why things are going so well in that house?" Jed had asked one night while we were lying in the bed of his truck.

"Why?" I turned to look at him.

"Because you agreed to their demands."

"What do you mean by that?"

"Well, remember back in 2013, our talk that night after your singing? The first one I went to."

"Yes," I replied.

"You said that night, one of his daughters told you and Phil that she didn't want you to write anymore books. That she thought you spent too much time on your computer? Then Phil told her you wouldn't be on your computer anymore if that would make the girls stay living with him. He decided that for you."

I nodded. That was true, and something that left a dagger in my soul. I was expected to remain unseen while handling all the cleaning and transportation duties. The expectation was for me to sacrifice my career and have no purpose. I had to sacrifice my identity to satisfy Phil and the girls. And right now, standing in this kitchen alone, cleaning up after everyone while they're all enjoying family time in the living room together, told me everything I needed to know.

I didn't belong to this family.

Chapter 25

Isabel

T hunder broke the silence as I lay in bed. I attempted to sleep, but the day's events became muddled in my mind. My life as I had known it was forever changed. My emotions ranged from sadness to nervousness and excitement. Yet I had this overwhelming feeling of wanting to cry.

I wished I could've met Zetta. I felt a sense of wonder as I read about her, her life, and being in her home. Despite the hardships she faced, she was an amazing woman. Throughout most of it, she had no say in or power over the situation. I guess that's what happens when you fall in love with the wrong person. It engulfs you and forces you to find your own way out of the abyss.

I wondered if Phil was still alive, or his girls. How horrible of them to treat her the way they did.

The cabin shook as another loud clap of thunder followed the flickering lights. I jolted awake in bed and stayed still. The rain and wind were picking up, and I crossed my fingers that the power wouldn't go out again.

I looked towards the closet and recalled a journal entry of Zetta's, about a box in her closet for me. I moved from the bed and into the closet, flipped on the light, and looked around.

I crouched on the floor and inspected the closet, looking behind clothing and shoes. As I passed her makeup station, my attention was drawn to a medium-sized gray tote tucked away in the back. I pulled it out, leaned against the shelves, and opened the box.

There were journals, photos, letters, and trinkets inside. I scanned the letters. Most of them were from New York. As I picked one letter from the envelope I instantly recognized my mom's handwriting, realizing they were letters to Zetta.

Every letter and photo my mother sent, Zetta had kept them all! I glanced at a few of my baby photos and couldn't help but smile. Some of these were new to me. I pulled out a photo album and opened the cover. More photos of me over the years.

What a hard thing to do, watching the child you gave up for adoption grow up in photos and letters.

I shook my head, realizing the strength she must have had. Having to live with Phil and his ungrateful daughters, and making the difficult decision to give up your own child to ensure their safety. Growing up with Zetta wouldn't have made a difference in how fulfilling my life turned out to be, even though I am thankful to her for giving me to my incredible parents. My childhood was truly amazing.

The lights flickered off as thunder roared once again. I put the lid on the box and pushed it to the side, then made my way to the kitchen to grab the flashlight.

I couldn't stop thinking about Zetta's photos displayed on the shelves in Weston's house. One photo of your favorite author, okay, but there were close to a dozen or more.

At the kitchen table I gazed into the darkness, my mind wandering.

I felt like there was something right in front of me I couldn't see. That it was clear as day, and I was just overlooking a very important piece of this puzzle. Like Zetta, I felt tossed into something I had no control over. Although I didn't have to deal with ungrateful people, there was something off.

As lightning flashed, I glanced at the table of journals and prepared for the impending thunder.

A powerful urge to go to Weston's house came over me as I glanced in that direction. I slipped into my shoes and stepped out into the middle of the storm.

Chapter 26

Zetta

Phil's pacing made me slump deeper into the couch. I knew I should've just left in silence and talked to him on the phone. Opting to confront him in person was not the right approach.

"I can't believe you! An affair?! With him?!" Phil's face was bright red, and I could tell he was thinking fast on how to shift the blame to me. "We've given you everything, Zetta. We've tried to make you happy, and no matter what the girls or I do, it will never be enough to make you happy."

That's it, I thought to myself as I shook my head. *There it is. I knew it was coming.*

"You have nothing to say?"

"I have a lot to say, Phil. A lot."

"Well, speak. The floor is all yours."

"My words don't matter. I have spent the last few years being who you and the girls want me to be—"

"That's bull!"

"Is it?" I replied. "When's the last time I've been able to write my books in my own home? Why is it that I have to drive hours to my cabin to write? Why do I have to support all the passions you all have, but none of you cares to support mine? It goes both ways."

"Both ways."

"Yes, Phil. Both ways. When is the last time you all attended an event with me? Or the last time we all went out to celebrate when my book hit number one on the list for the fourth week in a row? Or the—"

"You know, you just don't get it, do you?" He shook his head.

"I guess I don't. I guess I just misunderstood this entire relationship. Who is this person you want me to be? And the girls? Who is it they want me to be? It seems like if I stay quiet, all is good. But the minute I speak up, no matter what I say, it's wrong."

"That's not true, and you know it."

"Do you even know me, Phil?" I shook my head. "Really. Do you really know me? As in me?"

"What kind of question is that? You know what? You want a divorce, let's do it. I'm done with your games and—" He hesitated. "I'm just done with all of it. I'll sign the papers." He shook his head. "I can't believe you want to destroy this family once again. I never should've begged you to come back the last few times. Maybe I should've just let you go then. Then you could've spent all the time you wanted with him, and not have to go around behind my back for the last decade."

I shook my head. "The last decade? Really?"

"I know it's been going on longer than what you told me. You've changed these last few years. You're not the same charismatic, bubbly—"

"I've changed because you all want me to be

112

someone I'm not. I've already told you this. I'm done arguing about it. I'm leaving. I'm getting my life and myself back. I'll never go back to being whoever it was you wanted me to be. I'll have you know I love you, but I can't love your girls when they do anything and everything in their power to make me feel invisible."

He smirked and shook his head.

I walked out the door and never looked back. I cried driving back to the cabin, realizing the years I had wasted trying to please an ungrateful family. I had nothing to show from my entire time with Phil.

Nothing.

I was leaving with a blank slate before me. I was more upset with myself for staying so long in a place I didn't belong. The women in town were now free to discuss our divorce, spread gossip, and fabricate false narratives about what occurred. The truth would forever remain unknown to anyone.

No one would ever know what went on behind the door of that home. And I'd never speak on it ever again. It was over. It was really over.

I pulled into my driveway hours later and walked into the house.

This felt like home. This was my home.

"Hey." Jed smiled as he walked into the kitchen. "I thought I heard you walk in. How was the drive?" he asked as he embraced me.

"Good."

"And everything went well?"

"As well as it will ever get. I guess you should prepare yourself for the gossip now. If it wasn't loud enough then, it'll be plenty loud this time around."

"Aw, don't let them get to you. It's you and me now. Forever."

"Forever," I said as I kissed his lips.

"While you were gone, I finished up the bookshelves. Come check it out."

I followed him into the living room and gasped.

"Jed! It's gorgeous."

He moved closer to the bookcase. "I have one copy of all your hardcovers here." He beamed as he pointed to an area. "And I had to put a few photos of my favorite author out as well."

I laughed. "You don't need so many pictures of me out like that."

"Who else is going to see them? It's you and me here. And besides, when you're over there in your writing cabin it's nice to look up and see the woman I'm in love with on the shelf. I'd add more, but I thought that might be a little excessive."

"Well, this amount here looks excessive!" I laughed.

"A dozen is far from excessive."

Chapter 27

Isabel

I knocked aggressively on Weston's door. I remember him saying his doorbell wasn't working. The handle was locked when I tried it, so I resorted to pounding on the door once more. As the lightning flashed, a strong gust of wind soaked me with water. I fell against the door as the thunder rumbled.

I vigorously hammered on the door and screamed his name, hoping he could hear me over the thunder.

He answered the door. "Get inside!" he directed as he pulled me in and closed the door behind me. "What happened? Why are you out in the storm?"

"I have to see your bookshelf," I explained while catching my breath and attempting to dry my face with my wet arm.

"Let me grab a towel," he said as he went down a hallway.

I proceeded into the living room and walked towards the bookshelf with Zetta's books.

Weston returned to the room and placed a towel on my shoulders.

"What's going on?"

"I don't know yet," I replied.

"What do you mean you don't know?"

"Weston, I have something to tell you, but first I need to—" I stopped as I reached for a hardcover of Zetta's book and opened the cover. I flipped a few pages and glanced up at him.

"Who is—" I paused. "Who owns this house?"

"Um, like I said earlier—"

"I know what you said earlier. Jed?" I questioned him. "Is it Jed Conley?"

"How do you know that?"

"Oh God." I sighed as I closed the book and sat in the chair. "Oh—"

"Isabel, please tell me what's going on."

"When did he die?"

"July. Back in 2021. Why?"

"He's my father."

"What? He never had any kids."

"It's because she never had the chance to tell him before he died."

"Who?" he asked.

"My mother. Zetta."

"Your mother is Zetta Castellan?"

I nodded. "Yes. I just found that out yesterday. She gave me up for adoption after he ran off with some Claudia Tasley woman. And—"

"Whoa! Hold on here. You need to tell me the full story. I know Claudia."

"She stole Jed from Zetta. Well, pretty much interfered with their relationship years ago. Zetta went back to Phil when she learned that Jed was with Claudia."

"Who is Phil?"

"He doesn't matter anymore. But Zetta is my mother. Jed is my father. And now they're both dead and I never will get to meet either of them." I burst into tears as I placed the book on the table and wrapped the towel tighter around myself.

"Oh, Isabel. Well, I can tell you anything and everything you want to know about Jed. Like I said, he was like a father to me. And I was the son he never had. He was a great man. To be honest, you filled in a part of the story that I had been wondering about all these years."

"What's that?" I asked as I dried my eyes.

"He always talked about the woman who had his heart. And how he followed her success online and in articles. She was a writer. And I knew he loved to read, but I didn't realize just how much in love he was with her until a few years ago. I asked about her book and photos, and he would only smile and say nothing. But he held his hand over his heart and his entire face would light up. But he kept her a secret. It was like they had some sort of private relationship they never spoke of."

I tried to calm my crying as he spoke.

"Isabel, if he knew about you, he would've done everything in his power to find you and be a part of your life. That's the kind of man he was. True to his word, and up until his very last breath, the kindest soul that ever walked this earth."

"What do you know about Claudia?"

"She's a nice lady. I never had or heard of any issues with her."

"Did he see her often?"

"Jed? I guess. Again, I didn't know they had a relationship since she was married and had a family. You really think she had an affair with Jed all those years ago?"

I nodded. "Yes. Zetta talked often about driving past her house and seeing Jed's truck in the driveway. She also ran into them together in town, while out running errands. She saw them together a lot."

Weston nodded as he sat in the chair next to me.

"You think if Claudia never intervened, you'd have never been given up for adoption?"

"That exact thought is in my mind."

"Well, you can't change it, so try to not let it consume you. It's the past. And you can't change the past."

I nodded as I swallowed the lump in my throat. "I know. I just feel everything right now. This is overwhelming. I feel anger toward Claudia. That night, my mother—Zetta—" I paused. "That's the first time I've called her my mother," I grinned. "Feels so weird. But that night, she went to tell Jed she was pregnant. He was at Claudia's house."

Weston looked at me just as the lights flickered back on.

"And we have power." He smiled. "She never confronted Jed or Claudia?"

I shrugged my shoulders. "Not that I know of. I mean, Claudia emailed her to tell her to stay away from Jed. But I didn't see any response from Zetta."

"How do you know this?"

"I found the printed emails in a folder."

Weston paused. "You happen to have Zetta's log-ins for her email? Just because you don't have a printout doesn't mean she didn't respond."

I stared at him with wide eyes.

"I need to go back to the cabin. Now," I said as I placed my towel on the chair.

"I'll come with you," he said as he grabbed a coat and put it around me.

Chapter 28

Zetta

I haven't written in so long. Life has been a whirlwind. Beautiful and bittersweet. To live in the moment has been much-needed, and such a different way to live than I'm used to. I've struggled greatly to put into words this particular period of my life.

On July 23, 2021, Jed peacefully passed away in his sleep.

I'm in disbelief as I write these words. I hurt with the deepest hurt I've ever felt. This feels like a dream. Everything feels unreal. The man I've loved for decades, the father of my child, has been taken from me. Never again will I hear his laugh, see his smile, or feel him wrap his arms around me.

I don't know how to go on at this point. I've cancelled every event and put a hold on all my work. I'm confined to my bed, where I can only cling to his clothing and pillow, crying.

He's everywhere I look. And although I love it, it's killing me every second he's not here with me.

I'm truly alone in life.

I try to tend to his garden but all I do is cry. I can't move any of his things into this house. I want him back. Even for one more hour. There is so much we had planned. There is so much he wanted to do.

I hired some help with the yard. His name is Evan. All was well for one summer. He mistook my nice-ness for something else, and I had to let him go. But it didn't end well. He knew my routine and I would often find him lurking around my property. So I had cameras installed everywhere; a few phone calls to the police later, and I found myself in another small-town scandal.

I just want Jed back. I want my life back. I want to be left alone.

I never got the chance to tell Jed about our baby. Life was going smoothly, but keeping such a secret was hurting me too much to break the news to him. I suppose now he knows about her.

Life hasn't been good, but it hasn't been all that bad. These final years of life with Jed were the best years of my life. I feel like things happened the way they did for a reason. Jed wasn't ready to settle down back then. But he was when we met up again in 2013. Both of us needed to go through relationships to help us grow to love each other completely in the end. Me with Phil and him with Claudia.

Although she never showed up at the funeral, she sent a card.

How thoughtful.

I forgive her for what she did back then, too. She was the first person I reached out to for help when I was dealing with Phil's daughters. Rather than being the friend she claimed to be, she used my struggles against me by starting the rumors.

That was a hard lesson.

And then when I told her I was pregnant and needed to talk to Jed, she threatened to make all my issues public if I didn't leave him alone. I know where all the rumors started, and so does Claudia. But I'm not here to judge her. That's for someone else to do.

I don't know what else to say, other than I'm at a loss for words. This hurts.

I know if Jed were here with me right now, we'd be in each other's arms and he'd be holding me tight, whispering in my ear that everything is just fine.

Everything is not fine. Not even close. And since I can't write about anything else at the moment, I'm going to head back to my cabin for the night. I can't stand living in this house anymore.

I installed a fence to separate the properties.

I'm willing my cabin to our daughter.

The house will be willed to Weston Clark—the son we never had, but the young man who became like a son to Jed. It would be what Jed wanted.

Chapter 29

Isabel

Five Years Later

I grabbed another maroon sharpie from the cup as Weston put another stack of books onto the table.

"You're doing great!" He smiled.

I had been so nauseated the past few days leading up to today. It was the launch of my first book, and the true story of my mother, Zetta Castellan. It took a few years to piece it together and compile it into one book. It was a challenge, but we did it. I even added some photos of her in the middle of the book. It was the perfect touch; it's something she didn't want, but I feel she was gorgeous and needed to stop hiding that fact. Besides, I know she's proud of me.

Her story has been told. She can rest in peace.

"Meredith," the woman said as she handed me her book.

I glanced up and grinned. "Meredith! Oh, what a nice surprise to see you here."

She grinned and nodded. "I wouldn't miss this for the world. You've done an outstanding job."

"Well, thank you."

"Everything going well at the cabin?"

"Better than ever. Weston and I live in the house, and I use the cabin as my writing studio. Just like my mother did for those years."

It still felt strange to call Zetta my mother, but that's what she was.

I now know why I was chosen to write the story of Zetta Castellan. Everything and everyone in life has a purpose. Mine was to make my birth parents proud, and the added bonus was meeting Weston in the process.

I can only imagine how wonderful a man my father was. I've heard how much Weston takes after him, and it fills my heart with joy to hear that. Both of my parents were wonderful people.

"This just showed up for you. Some lady dropped it off and said she couldn't stay," Catherine, my new assistant said as she set an envelope on the table.

"What is it?" Weston queried as he sat down next to me.

I signed the last book and proceeded to open the manila envelope. I pulled out a stack of opened letters addressed to Jed Conley. As I pulled one of the letters from inside the envelope, I already knew the handwriting.

These were the letters that Zetta had written to Jed when she couldn't get a hold of him on the phone after Claudia had her number blocked.

"Who dropped these off?" I asked Catherine.

"An older blonde lady."

I glanced at Weston.

"Claudia," we said in unison.

"I can't believe she had these. She really did try her hardest to keep them apart."

"Well, looks like you have to write a part two to the book now." Weston smiled. "Claudia returns and the mysteriously lost letters show up."

"I just wish I could write the story with a happy ending."

"It does have a happy ending," he said. "All these roads led us to each other. And I really feel like we had guidance from your parents in this. They wanted us to live the life of love that they never got the chance to."

I smiled at him.

"Well?" He smiled. "You can't tell me we would've found our way to each other if this all didn't happen. You living in New York and me living in a small town in Wisconsin. Think about it."

I knew he was right. This story did have a happy ending. I reached for his hand as he wrapped me in his arms.

THE END

Thank You!

Thank you very much for reading THE GHOST-WRITER. If you enjoyed this story and would like to stay updated with all the Kaira Lockwood books, please subscribe to my free newsletter by visiting my website: www.kairalockwood.com

Mom,

I don't even know where to begin. I don't know you, but I miss you. I'm trying hard to keep my head above water, but I feel like I'm drowning from all the tears I still have yet to cry.

I don't know how to grieve the loss of you. Or, how to grieve the life we lost out on. I'm confused.

I feel like I have no one to talk to about this. It's hard for me to put into perspective all that I have learned from you and about you.

I feel angry.
Angry at Phil.
Hatred toward his kids. That I don't even know.
And, I'm not sure what to think about my own father.

And don't even get me started on Claudia.

I'm glad I have Weston to lean on. At least he understands and in a strange sort of way, we're grieving for the same loss. He tells me about my father all the time. Although, I'm hurt by what he did to you, he does seem like he was a great man.

I often wonder the same thoughts you had. What if Claudia was never in the picture? Weston and I talk about that a lot. If life had happened that way, I never would've met him. And he's the best thing that's happened to me in life.

So, did things go the way they did, because that's was the universe had planned? I have so many questions.

I just hope I make both you and dad proud. I hope both Weston and I do.

I decided to follow in your footsteps and write books. I resigned from my position in the city. It felt like the right thing to do. I'm happy with the decision.

My first book about your life story sold well. The publisher wants to sign on two more books. Weston and I are taking time to plan out and see if this is possible.

I don't know a lot about dad, but Weston does.

Oh, and another thing.

All those letters you wrote dad over the years. Some are opened and some are still sealed. I'm sure you already know Claudia was at my signing, and dropped them off.

I'm assuming she hid them from him.

I've been reading your letters, and they make me cry. I can only get through one or two of them at a time.

If only dad knew how much you loved him, and begged for him to reach out to you. If only he knew a lot of things. But it's heartbreaking.

I can't imagine living life with half a heart – like you mentioned often in your letters.

I promise I'll try and get over my hatred towards those that interfered with your life on purpose, and made it a living hell. I'm trying to learn forgiveness like you talk about often in your journals. But it's hard.

It gives me peace knowing that you did find happiness with dad. Even if it was for such a short while, at least you were given the chance to experience those moments. And both of you were able To be together in the end.

Weston and I have been taking good care of the property and both the house and the cabin. We decided against making changes and want to keep it just as you both left things. In a way, it makes him feel closer to dad, and I feel closer to you.

I know dad was a great man. When Weston tells me stories about him, he cries. And then I cry. Before you know it, we're both crying.

And then we laugh-cry, if that's what you call it. He has so many wonderful stories to tell. And I read him entries from your journals that I think he'll find interesting. Don't worry. I keep the secret stuff, secret.

I've been thinking a lot about your life, and it's

intriguing. When I try and place your letters to dad to correspond with your journal entries. I'm starting to see your life in a new perspective. I know you had challenges and things happen beyond your control. I only hope I can be as strong as you had to be.

I'll write more later, but I want to thank you for giving me life. And for leaving me this legacy to continue. I will make you proud. I promise.

And one day, when we have little ones, I hope I can pass this on down to my own daughter.

I love you, mom.

Forever Yours!
Isabel